'This was not meant to happen.'

'So let me go,' said Rosa a little breathlessly, not entirely immune to the appeal of those emerald-green eyes, no matter what he'd said.

This close she could also see that silvery scar she'd noticed earlier. She quivered in spite of herself. How had he really got that?

'Yeah, I should,' he agreed, distracting her, his gaze dwelling on her mouth with an intensity that felt practically physical. 'But you know what?' He shifted against her and she was almost sure she could feel him hardening. 'I don't want to. Now, isn't that the damnedest thing?'

New York Times bestselling author **Anne Mather** has written since she was seven, but it was only when her first child was born that she fulfilled her dream of becoming a writer. Her first book, CAROLINE, appeared in 1966. It met with immediate success, and since then Anne has written more than 140 novels, reaching a readership which spans the world.

Born and raised in the north of England, Anne still makes her home there with her husband, two children and, now, grandchildren. Asked if she finds writing a lonely occupation, she replies that her characters always keep her company. In fact, she is so busy sorting out their lives that she often doesn't have time for her own! An avid reader herself, she devours everything from sagas and romances to mainstream fiction and suspense. Anne has also written a number of mainstream novels, with DANGEROUS TEMPTATION, her most recent title, published by MIRA® Books.

STAY THROUGH THE NIGHT

BY
ANNE MATHER

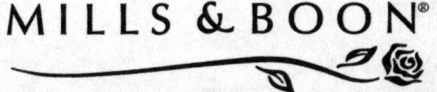

MILLS & BOON®

First published in Great Britain 2006
Harlequin Mills & Boon Limited,
Eton House, 18-24 Paradise Road, Richmond, Surrey TW9 1SR

© Anne Mather 2006

ISBN-13: 978 0 263 84842 7
ISBN-10:   0 263 84842 6

Set in Times Roman 10½ on 12¾ pt.
01-0906-48607

Printed and bound in Spain
by Litografia Rosés, S.A., Barcelona

STAY THROUGH
THE NIGHT

CHAPTER ONE

IT WAS COLD. Much colder than Rosa had expected, actually. When she'd arrived the night before, she'd put the cold down to the drizzling rain, to her own feelings of anxiety and apprehension. But this morning, after a reasonably good night's rest and a bowl of Scottish porridge for breakfast, she didn't have any excuses.

Where was the heatwave that was supposed to sweep all of the UK through July and August? Not here in Mallaig, that was definite, and Rosa glanced back at the cosy lounge of the bed and breakfast where she'd spent the night with real regret.

Of course part of that unwillingness to part with familiar things was the knowledge that in the next few hours she was going to be stepping into totally unknown territory. An island, some two hours off the coast of Scotland, was not like visiting some local estate. That was why she was here in Mallaig, which was the ferry port for the Western Isles. In an hour she'd be boarding the boat—*ship*?—that would take her to Kilfoil, and she still didn't know if that was where Sophie was.

Fortunately, she'd brought some warm clothes with her, and this morning she had layered herself with a vest, a shirt and a woollen sweater. Feeling the chill wind blowing off the water, she guessed she'd have to wear her cashmere jacket as well for the crossing to the island. She just wished she'd packed her leather coat. It was longer and would have kept her legs warm.

Still, at least it was fine, and she could survive for two hours, she told herself, leaving the guesthouse behind and walking down the narrow main street to the docks. Crossing the already busy car parking area, she went to the end of the jetty, wrapping her arms about herself as she gazed out over the water.

For all it was cold, the view was outstandingly beautiful. The island of Skye was just a short distance away, and she wondered if those purple-tipped mountains she could see were the famous Cuillins. She didn't know. In fact she knew very little about this part of Scotland. Despite the fact that her grandfather Ferrara had been imprisoned near Edinburgh during the war, she had never been farther north than Glasgow. She did have aunts and uncles and cousins there, but her visits had been few and far between.

Now, she realised she should have been more adventurous when she had the chance. But she'd gone to college in England, married an English boy and lived in Yorkshire for most of her life to date. It was easy to make the excuse that she hadn't ventured very far because of her widowed mother and younger sister. But the truth was she wasn't an adventurous sort of person, and Colin had always been happiest spending holidays in Spain, where he could get a tan.

Of course she couldn't make Colin an excuse any longer. Three years ago, when she'd discovered he'd been cheating on her with his boss's secretary, Rosa hadn't hesitated before asking for a divorce. Colin had begged her to reconsider, had said that she couldn't destroy five years of marriage over one solitary lapse. But Rosa knew it hadn't only been a solitary lapse. It wasn't the first time she'd suspected him of seeing someone else, and she doubted it would be the last.

Fortunately—or unfortunately, as far as Rosa was concerned—they'd had no children to be hurt by the break-up. Rosa didn't know if it was her fault or Colin's, but she'd never been pregnant. Of course during the turmoil of the divorce Colin had blamed her for his unfaithfulness. If she'd spent more time with him, he said, and less at that damn school with kids who didn't appreciate her, their marriage might have stood a chance. But Rosa knew that was only an excuse. Without her salary as an English teacher Colin would not have been able to afford the frequent trips to the continent that he so enjoyed.

Anyway, it was all in the past now, she thought ruefully. And, although sometimes the things Colin had done still hurt a little, on the whole she was getting on with her life. That was until the phone call yesterday morning that had brought her on this possibly wild goose chase to Kilfoil. But her mother had been desperate, and frantic with worry, and Rosa had known she had no choice but to do as she wished.

She sighed, resting her hands on the bars of the railings, staring out across the water as if the view might provide the answers she sought. What if her mother was wrong? What if Sophie wasn't on the island? Would there be some kind of inn or hostelry there where she could spend the night until the ferry returned the following day?

She'd been told the ferry booking office opened at nine o'clock, and that she should have no trouble getting a ticket to Kilfoil. Apparently the majority of the traffic from

Mallaig was between there and Armadale, the small port on Skye where they all disembarked.

But that wasn't the ferry Rosa needed. She would be boarding the one taking tourists and backpackers to islands farther afield. Dear God, she thought, it sounded so remote, so inaccessible. For the first time she half wished her mother had come with her. It would be so good to have someone she knew to talk to.

Liam drove the Audi into the car park and swung his legs out of the car. Then, holding on to the roof with one hand and the top of the door with the other, he hauled himself to his feet and looked around.

The wind off the water was knife-sharp, but he didn't notice it. He'd been born in Hampstead, but he'd lived in Scotland for the past ten years. Ever since his first book had been such an astounding success, actually, and he was used to the climate. A famous Hollywood director had read his book and liked it, and had optioned it for the iconic blockbuster it had become. But that had been when his life in London had gradually—and ultimately violently—become impossible to sustain.

He ran a hand down over his thigh, feeling the ridge of hard flesh that arced down into his groin even through his worn jeans. He'd been lucky, he reflected. Of the many wounds he'd had that one could have killed him. Instead, although the knife had severed his femoral artery, causing an almost fatal loss of blood, and sliced through enough nerves and sinews to leave him with a permanent weakness in his left leg, he'd survived. It was his attacker who'd died, turning the knife on himself when he'd been confident he'd achieved his objective.

Liam grimaced, determinedly shoving such thoughts aside. It had all happened a long time ago now, and since then none of his books had aroused such a frenzied response in his readers. He took a deep breath of cold sea air, glad that he'd chosen to drive back from London overnight to catch this morning's ferry to the island. There wouldn't be another ferry until Thursday, and he was impatient to get back to Kilfoil and to his work.

Locking the car, he flexed his shoulder muscles and stretched his legs, feeling the stiffness of driving almost non-stop for ten hours in his bones. He had pulled off into a service area around 3:00 a.m. for coffee, and slept for twenty minutes before resuming his journey. But it wasn't the same as sleeping in his bed.

His attention was caught by the sight of a lone woman leaning on the railings at the end of the jetty. It was her hair that had drawn his eyes: deep red and wildly curly, it refused to be controlled by the ribbon she'd tied at her nape. But she seemed hardly aware of it. She was gazing out towards Skye, as if she hoped to find some kind of answer in the mist gathering over the rain-shrouded hills.

Liam shrugged. She was obviously a visitor, dressed for summer in the Highlands, he thought ironically. But, while they had been known to have temperatures well into the eighties, at present the northerly breeze was creating a more predictable sixty-five.

Jack Macleod, who ran a fleet of sailboats that he hired out to tourists, hailed Liam as he left the car and started across to the ferry terminal. 'Now, then, stranger,' he said, grinning broadly. 'We were beginning to think you'd changed your mind about coming back.'

'You can't get rid of me that easily,' said Liam, hooking

his thumbs into the back pockets of his jeans, his chambray shirt parting at the neck to reveal the dark hair clustered at his throat. 'I got back as soon as I could. Spending too long in overcrowded cities doesn't appeal to me any more.'

'Didn't I hear you'd gone to London to see the medic?' Jack asked, regarding his friend with critical eyes. 'Nothing serious, I hope.'

'A check-up, that's all,' said Liam quickly, not wanting to discuss his private affairs in public. He was aware that their voices had attracted the attention of the woman at the quayside, and she was looking at them over her shoulder.

She sensed their awareness of her interest and looked away, but not before Liam had registered an oval face and unusually dark eyes for a woman of her colouring. Of course her hair colouring might not be natural, which was probably the case, and although she was tall she was much too thin.

'You'll be getting this morning's ferry,' Jack was continuing, unaware of Liam's distraction, and he forced himself to concentrate on what the man had said.

'If I can,' he agreed, accepting Jack's assurances that Angus Gallagher would never turn him away, and when he looked back towards the jetty the woman was gone.

Rosa went back to the bed and breakfast, collected her things and was back at the terminal building in time to book her passage to Kilfoil. She supposed she looked like any other tourist, in her jeans and trainers, with a backpack over her shoulder. The other backpackers, queuing for their tickets, didn't give her a second glance. Unlike the two men she'd seen earlier in the car park. Well, one of them, anyway. He'd certainly given her a thorough appraisal.

And found her wanting, she was sure. She'd definitely

sensed his disapproval. But whether that was because he'd found her watching them, she couldn't be absolutely sure.

Whatever, he had been attractive, she conceded, remembering his height—well over six feet, she estimated—and the broad shoulders filling out his crumpled shirt. She guessed he was one of the fishermen who, in increasingly smaller numbers, trawled these waters. He hadn't looked like a tourist, and the man who had been with him had been wearing waders, she thought.

Still, she was unlikely to see either of them again—unless one of them was the captain of the vessel she was hoping to sail on. Maybe someone on the ferry would remember a pretty blond girl travelling out to Kilfoil the previous week. Dared she ask about Liam Jameson? She didn't think so. According to his publicity, the man was reputed to be a recluse, for goodness' sake. So why had he been attending a pop festival in Glastonbury? For research? She didn't think so.

Her mind boggled, as it always did when she thought about what her mother had told her. Sophie had pulled some stunts before, but nothing remotely resembling this. Rosa had thought her sister was settling down at last, that she and Mark Campion might move in together. But now that relationship was all up in the air because of some man Sophie had met during the pop festival.

Rosa got her ticket and moved outside again. The rain that had been threatening earlier seemed to be lifting, and the sun was actually shining on the loch. A good omen, she thought, looking about her for the ferry she'd been told would be departing in three-quarters of an hour. Pedestrian passengers would be embarked first, before the vehicles that would drive straight onto the holding deck.

She saw the man again as she was waiting in line at the quayside. He had driven his car round to join the queue of traffic waiting to board. Unexpectedly, her pulse quickened. So he was taking the same ferry she was. What a coincidence. But it was unlikely he was going to Kilfoil. According to Mrs Harris at the guesthouse, Kilfoil had been deserted for several years before a rich writer had bought the property and restored the ruined castle there for his own use.

Liam Jameson, of course, Rosa had concluded, unwilling to press the landlady for too many details in case she betrayed the real reason why she was going to the island. She'd told her that she planned to photograph the area for an article she was writing on island development. But Mrs Harris had warned her that the island was private property and she would have to get permission to take photographs.

She lost sight of the man when she and her fellow passengers went to board the ferry. Climbing the steep steps to the upper deck, Rosa shivered as the wind cut through even her cashmere jacket. God, she thought, why would anyone choose to live here if they had the money to buy an island? Barbados, yes. The Caymans, maybe. But Kilfoil? He had to be crazy!

Still, she could only assume it gave him atmosphere for his horror stories. And, according to her sister, they were shooting his latest movie on the island itself. But was that feasible? Had the story Sophie had told Mark any truth in it at all? Rosa wouldn't have thought so, but her mother had believed every word.

If only Jameson hadn't involved Sophie, she thought unhappily. At almost eighteen, her sister was terribly impressionable, and becoming a professional actress was her ambition. But although she always maintained she was old enough to make her own decisions, she'd made plenty of bad ones in the past.

If she had met Jameson she would have been impressed, no question about it. His books sold in the millions. For heaven's sake, Sophie devoured every new one as soon as it came out. And all his films to date had been box office successes. His work had acquired a cult status, due to an increasing fascination with the supernatural. Particularly vampires—which were his trademark.

But would he have been attending a rock festival? Stranger things had happened, she supposed, and Sophie had certainly convinced Mark that this was a chance she couldn't miss. Why she hadn't phoned her mother and told her, why she'd left Mark to make her excuses, was less convincing. But if she had been lying, where in God's name was she?

Thankfully, there was a cabin on the upper deck where passengers could buy sandwiches, sodas and hot drinks once the ferry sailed. Rosa stepped inside gratefully, finding herself a seat near the window so she could watch the comings and goings on the dock.

It didn't take long to board the remaining passengers, and the queue of automobiles soon disappeared below. They must be loaded in the order they would disembark, Rosa reflected, wondering if the man she'd seen was familiar with the routine.

The ferry was due to sail to Kilfoil first, then the other islands on its schedule. Rosa was glad. It meant that Kilfoil was the nearest, and as the boat slipped its mooring lines and moved out into the sea loch she hoped it wouldn't be too far.

The island of Skye seemed incredibly close as they

started on their journey, and for a while other islands hemmed them in, giving an illusion of intimacy. But then the body of water widened and the swell caused the small vessel to rise and fall more heavily on the waves.

Rosa hunched her shoulders and glanced back at the group of people gathered at the snack bar. She wished she'd bought herself a drink before it got busy. As it was, she wasn't totally sure she could walk across the cabin without becoming nauseous. She'd never been a good sailor, and the bucking ferry was much worse than the hovercraft she and Colin had once taken to Boulogne.

'Are you feeling okay?'

Guessing she must be looking pale, Rosa turned her head and found the man from the car park looking down at her. So he *had* boarded this ferry, she thought inconsequentially, noticing that the rolling vessel didn't seem to bother him. Apart from donning a well-worn leather jacket over his shirt and jeans, he looked just as big and powerful as she'd thought earlier. The shirt pulled away from the tight jeans in places, to expose a wedge of hair-roughened brown skin.

Sex on legs, she mused, momentarily diverted from her troubles, but he was waiting for an answer and she forced a rueful smile. 'I didn't expect it to be so rough,' she confessed, wondering if he was aware that her eyes were on a level with his groin. She endeavoured to look anywhere else than there. 'I suppose you're used to it?'

His eyes narrowed, thick black lashes veiling irises that were a clear emerald-green. God, he was good-looking, she thought, noting his tanned skin, his firm jaw and his mouth, which was oddly sensual despite being compressed into a thin line. But then he spoke again, his voice harder than

before, and she was diverted from her thoughts by the realisation that he didn't have a Scottish accent.

'Why do you say that?' he demanded, and Rosa blinked,
unable for a moment to remember exactly what she had said.

But then it came back to her. 'Um—I just thought you
seemed familiar with the area,' she confessed awkwardly,
wondering what was wrong with that. 'Evidently I was
mistaken. You're English, aren't you?'

Liam scowled, cursing himself for the impulse that had
driven him to ask if she was all right. She'd looked so
damned pale he'd felt sorry for her. She was obviously out
of place here. No waterproof clothing, no boots, even the
pack she'd dumped beside her looked flimsy.

'We don't all speak the Gaelic,' he said at last, and she
shrugged her slim shoulders.

'Okay.' Rosa quelled her indignation. At least their conversation was distracting her eyes from the restless sea
outside. 'So,' she said at last, 'do you live in the islands?'

'Perhaps.' He was annoyingly reticent. And then, discon-
certingly, 'I hope you don't intend to go hiking in that outfit.'

Rosa gasped. 'Not that it's any of your business.'

'No,' he conceded ruefully. 'I was just thinking out loud.
But I couldn't help noticing how cold you looked earlier.'

So he *had* noticed her. Rosa felt a little less antagonistic towards him. 'It is much colder than I'd anticipated,' she
admitted. 'But I don't expect to be here long.'

'Just a flying visit?'

'Something like that.'

Liam frowned. 'You've got relatives here?'

Rosa caught her breath. He certainly asked a lot of questions. But then she remembered she'd been going to ask if
anyone had seen her sister. If this man used the ferry on a

regular basis, he might have seen her. And Liam Jameson. But she preferred not to mention him.

'As a matter of fact, I'm hoping to catch up with my sister,' she said, trying to sound casual. 'A pretty blond girl. I believe she made this crossing a couple of days ago.'

'She can't have,' he said at once. 'This ferry only leaves every Monday and Thursday. If she made the crossing at all, it had to have been last Thursday.'

Rosa swallowed. Last Thursday Sophie had still been in Glastonbury with Mark. It had been on Saturday night that he'd phoned to tell her mother what had happened, and that had resulted in Mrs Chantry phoning Rosa in such an hysterical state.

'Are you sure?' she asked now, trying to assimilate what she'd learned, wondering if Liam Jameson had a plane or a helicopter. He probably did, she thought. Why should he travel with the common herd? He might even have a boat that he kept at Mallaig. It had probably been naïve of her to think otherwise.

'I'm sure,' her companion replied, his gaze considering. 'Does this mean you don't think your sister's here, after all?'

'Maybe.' Rosa had no intention of sharing her thoughts with him. She took a deep breath. 'Is it much farther, do you know?'

'That depends where you're going,' said Liam drily, curious in spite of himself, and Rosa decided there was no harm in telling him her destination.

'Um—Kilfoil,' she said, aware that her words had surprised him. Well, let him stew, she thought defiantly. He hadn't exactly been candid with her.

CHAPTER TWO

LIAM WAS SURPRISED. He'd thought he knew everything about the families who had moved to the island after he'd first acquired it. Having been uninhabited for several years, the cottages had fallen into disrepair, and it had taken a communal effort on all their parts to make the place viable again. In the process of rewiring the cottages, reconnecting the electric generator and generally providing basic services, they'd become his friends as well as his tenants. These days Kilfoil had a fairly buoyant economy, with tourism, fishing and farming giving a living to about a hundred souls.

He wanted to ask why she thought her sister might be on the island, but he knew he'd asked too many questions already. Okay, she intrigued him, with her air of shy defiance and the innocence with which she spoke of his island. Unless he missed his guess, there was something more than a desire to catch up with her sister here. Had the girl run away? Or eloped, maybe, with a boyfriend? But why would she come to Kilfoil? As far as he was aware, there was no regular minister on the island.

Rosa saw him push his hands into the back pockets of his jeans, apparently unaware that the button at his waist had come undone. She was tempted to tell him, except that

that would reveal where she was looking, and she hurriedly averted her head.

'About another hour,' he said, answering her question, and then, as if sensing her withdrawal, he moved away to approach the bar at the other end of the cabin. It was quiet now, and, watching with covert eyes, she saw him speak to the young man who was serving. Money changed hands, and then the young man pushed two polystyrene cups across the counter.

Two?

Rosa looked quickly away. Was one for her? She dared not look, dared not watch him walk back to where she was sitting in case she was mistaken.

'D'you want a coffee?'

But no. He was standing right in front of her again. 'Oh—um—you shouldn't have,' she mumbled awkwardly, but she took the cup anyway. 'Thanks.' She levered off the plastic lid and tasted it. 'Why don't you sit down?'

Liam hesitated now. This wasn't his usual practice, buying strange women cups of coffee, letting them share his space. But she looked so out of place here he couldn't abandon her. She might be a journalist, he reflected, eager to get a story. But, if so, she'd been very offhand with him.

Nevertheless, she seemed far too vulnerable to be alone, and much against his better judgement he dropped down into the empty seat beside her. Opening his own coffee, he cast a sideways glance in her direction. Then he saw her watching him and said hastily, 'At least it's hot.'

'It's very nice,' Rosa assured him, not altogether truthfully. The coffee was bitter. 'It was kind of you to get it for me.'

Liam shrugged. 'Scottish hospitality,' he said wryly. 'We're well known for it.'

She gave him a sideways look. 'So you *are* Scottish?' she said. 'You must know this area very well.' She paused. 'What's Kilfoil like? Is it very uncivilised?'

Liam caught his breath, almost choking on a mouthful of coffee. 'Where do you think you are?' he exclaimed, when he could speak again. 'The wilds of Outer Mongolia?'

'No.' Despite herself, her cheeks burned. 'So tell me about the island. Are there houses, shops, hotels?'

Liam hesitated, torn between the desire to describe his home in glowing detail and the urge not to appear too familiar with his surroundings. 'It's like a lot of the other islands,' he said at last. 'There's a village, and you can buy most of the staple things you need there. The post and luxury items come in on the ferry. As do the tourists, who stay at the local guesthouses.'

Rosa felt relieved. 'So it's not, like—desolate or anything?'

'It's beautiful,' said Liam, thinking how relieved he'd be to be back again. 'All these islands are beautiful. I wouldn't live anywhere else.'

Rosa's brows arched. 'Where do you live?'

He was cornered. 'On Kilfoil,' he said reluctantly. And then, deciding he'd said quite enough, he got to his feet again. 'Excuse me. I need to go and check on my car.'

When he'd gone, Rosa finished her coffee thoughtfully. She wasn't totally surprised by his answer, but she couldn't help wondering what a man like him found to do there. Could he be a fisherman, as she'd speculated? Somehow that didn't seem very likely. A thought occurred to her. Perhaps he worked for Liam Jameson. Or the film crew, if they were making a film on the island.

She should have asked if there was a film crew on the

island, she chided herself. But then, if she had, she'd have had to explain why she was really here. No, it was wiser to wait until she got there before she started asking those questions. She didn't want to alert Jameson as to who she was.

She couldn't help the shudder that passed over her at the thought of what she had to do. Her *mission*, she thought wryly. Goodness, what was she letting herself in for? But surely if there was a film crew on the island the people in the village would know about it. Whether they'd tell her where Liam Jameson lived was another matter.

The journey seemed endless, even worse than the three train journeys she'd had to make to get to Mallaig. Then at least she'd had some scenery to look at. Apart from a handful of mist-strewn islands, all she could see now was the choppy water lapping at the sides of the ferry.

She sighed and glanced at her watch. If what the man had said was true, it shouldn't be long now. Glancing towards the front of the vessel, she glimpsed a solid mass of land immediately ahead of them. Was that Kilfoil? She hoped so. She'd call her mother as soon as she stepped onto dry land.

Lucia Chantry would be desperate for news. Sophie was her baby, and although she knew as well as anyone that her daughter could be selfish and willful at times, Rosa had never been left in any doubt as to who was her mother's favourite. Sophie could do no wrong, whereas Rosa was constantly making mistakes. Not least when she'd married Colin Vincent. Her mother had never liked him, and she hadn't hesitated to say *I told you so* when Colin turned out to be such a jerk.

The ferry was slowing now, cutting back on its engines, preparing for its arrival at Kilfoil. As it eased into its berth,

Rosa got to her feet, eager for her first glimpse of her destination. It was certainly unprepossessing, she thought, just a handful of cottages climbing up the hillside from the ferry terminal. But the overcast sky didn't help. She was sure it would look much more appealing in sunlight.

Fifteen minutes later she was standing on the quay, watching as the few cars heading for the island rolled off the ferry. Glancing about her, she saw the road that wound up out of the village and the dark slopes of a mountain range behind.

The island suddenly seemed much bigger than she'd anticipated. But what had she been expecting? Something the size of Holy Island, off the coast of Northumberland, perhaps? And if she did find Sophie here, if she hadn't been lying, how was she supposed to get her to come home? If her sister was starstruck, she wouldn't be influenced by anything Rosa said.

Rosa had just located a sign that said 'Post Office' when she saw a dusty grey Audi coming up the ramp towards her. The man who'd bought her coffee was at the wheel and she turned abruptly away. She didn't want him to think—even for a moment—that she was looking for him.

To her relief, the big car swept past her, but then it braked hard, just a dozen yards up the road, and she saw its reversing lights appear. It stopped beside her and a door was pushed open. The man thrust his legs out, got to his feet with an obvious effort and turned towards her.

She noticed he was favouring his left leg, something she hadn't observed on the ferry. But then, the rolling of the vessel would have precluded any observation of that kind. She'd been decidedly unsteady on her own feet.

Liam, meanwhile, was cursing himself for being all

kinds of an idiot for stopping the car. But, dammit, she still looked as if a puff of wind would blow her away. And she certainly wasn't interested in him. He'd noticed the way she'd deliberately turned her back on him. So what was he doing playing the knight errant again?

'Got a problem?' he asked, forcing her to turn and face him.

'I hope not,' she said tightly, wishing he would just go away. But, on the off-chance that he might be able to help her, she ought to be more grateful. 'Um—I was looking for the Post Office, that's all. I wanted to ask where Kilfoil Castle was.'

'Kilfoil Castle?' Liam was wary now. 'Why do you want to know where Kilfoil Castle is? It's not open to the public, you know.'

'I know that.' Rosa sighed. Then, giving in to the urge to trust him, she added, 'Do you happen to know if there's a film crew working there?'

'A film crew?' Now Liam was genuinely concerned. Had he been wrong about this woman all along?

'Yes, a film crew,' repeated Rosa. 'I understand they're making a film of one of the Liam Jameson's books on the island.'

Like hell!

Liam stared at her, trying to decide if she was as naïve as she looked. 'Why would you imagine Liam Jameson would allow a film crew to desecrate his home?' he demanded bleakly. 'Movies have been made of his books, I know, but they're not filmed *here*.'

Was it just his imagination or did her shoulders sag at this news? What was going on, for God's sake? Had she expected to find her sister on the set? 'I think you've made a mistake,' he said gently. 'Someone's given you the wrong information. I can assure you there's no production team at Kilfoil Castle or anywhere else on the island.'

Rosa shook her head. 'Are you sure?'

'I'm sure.'

'You're not just trying to put me off?'

'Hell, no!' Liam gazed at her compassionately. 'I realise it must be a blow, but I don't think your sister's here.'

Rosa's brows drew together. 'I don't remember saying that I thought my sister was with the film crew,' she retorted defensively.

'No, but it doesn't take a mathematician to put two and two together.'

Rosa bit her lip. 'All right. Perhaps I did think Sophie might be with them. But if she's not, then perhaps she's somewhere else.'

Liam gazed at her. 'On the island?'

'Yes.' Rosa held up her head. 'So perhaps you could direct me to Kilfoil Castle, as I asked before. Is there a taxi or something I could hire if it's too far to walk?'

Liam blinked. 'Why on earth would you think your sister might be at Kilfoil Castle?' he asked, trying not to sound outraged at the suggestion, and his companion sighed.

'Because she apparently met Liam Jameson a few days ago, at the pop festival in Glastonbury. He told her they were making a film of his latest book in Scotland and he offered her a screen test.'

To say Liam was stunned would have been a vast understatement. It was as if she'd suddenly started talking in a foreign language and he couldn't make head or tail of what she was saying. For goodness' sake, until Sunday morning he'd been in a London clinic having muscle therapy to try and ease the spasms he still suffered in his leg. Besides which, he'd never been to a pop festival in his life.

Realising she was waiting for him to say something, Liam tried to concentrate. It was obvious she believed what she'd just told him. Her look of uncertainty and expectation was too convincing to fake. But, dammit, if her sister had fed her this story, why had she believed it? Anyone who knew Liam Jameson would know it was untrue.

But perhaps she didn't. Certainly she hadn't recognised him. And, taken at face value, it wasn't so outrageous. Two of his books *had* been filmed in Scotland. But not on Kilfoil. He'd made damn sure of that.

'Liam Jameson does live here, doesn't he?'

Rosa was wishing he'd say something, instead of just staring at her with those piercing green eyes. They seemed to see into her soul, and she shifted a little uncomfortably under their intent appraisal. He probably wasn't aware of it, but they were making her feel decidedly hot.

'Yes,' he said at last, when she'd finally managed to drag her gaze away from his. 'Yes, he lives at Kilfoil Castle, as I assume you know. But there's no way he could offer your sister a screen test. He isn't involved in film production. If she told you he was, she was wrong.'

'How do you know?' Although Rosa was prepared to accept that he might be right, she was curious how he could be so certain about it. 'Do you know him personally?'

Liam had been expecting that. 'I know of him,' he said, curiously reluctant to tell her who he was. 'He's— something of a recluse, and to my knowledge he's never been to Glastonbury. Your sister sounds quite young. Jameson is forty-two.'

'Forty-two!' If he'd expected her to know his age, too, he'd been mistaken. She hunched her shoulders. 'That old?'

'It's not so old,' muttered Liam, unable to prevent a twinge of indignation. 'How old is your sister?'

'Almost eighteen,' answered Rosa at once. 'Do you think Liam Jameson likes young girls?'

'He's not a pervert,' said Liam sharply, and then modified his tone as he continued, 'And, let's face it, you don't have any proof that it was Jameson she went off with.'

'I know.' Rosa blew out a breath. 'But where else can she be?' She wet her lips, her tongue moving with unknowing provocation over their soft contours. 'Anyway, if you'll give me those directions to the castle, I'll go and see if Mr Jameson has an answer.'

That was when Liam should have stopped her. He should have explained who he was, and how he knew Jameson had never been to Glastonbury, but he chickened out. He'd gone too far with the deception to simply confess that he was the man she was looking for. And his innate sense of privacy made him a victim of his own deceit.

'Look, I think you're wasting your time,' he said carefully. 'Jameson has never been to a pop festival.' He caught her eyes on him. 'As far as I know.'

'You know an awful lot about him,' said Rosa curiously. 'Are you sure you're not a friend of his?'

'I'm sure,' said Liam, wishing he'd never started this. 'But I do live on the island. It's a small place.'

'It doesn't seem very small,' said Rosa unhappily. 'And I'm not really looking forward to meeting this man, if you want the truth. He writes about horrible things. Ghosts and werewolves—'

'Vampires,' put in Liam unthinkingly.

'—stuff like that,' she muttered, proving she hadn't been listening to him. 'That's probably why Sophie was so impressed by him. She's read everything he's ever written.'

'Really?'

Liam couldn't help feeling a glow of satisfaction. No matter how often he was told by his agent or his publisher that he was a good writer, he never truly believed it.

'Oh, yes.' Rosa sighed again. 'Sophie's mad on books and TV and movies. She wants to be an actress, you see. If this man has been in contact with her, she'll be like putty in his hands.'

'But he hasn't,' said Liam. And then he amended that to, 'You don't really believe he has?'

'Perhaps not.' Rosa had to be honest. 'But, if you don't mind, I'd rather hear that from Liam Jameson himself.'

Liam scowled, scuffing the toe of his boot against a stone, aware that at any moment someone could come up and speak to him and then he wouldn't have any choice in the matter.

'Look,' he said reluctantly. 'Why don't you just get on the ferry again and go home? If your sister wants to tell you where she is, she will. Until then, it would probably be wiser for you not to accuse people of things you can't know or prove.'

Rosa shivered. 'Get on the ferry again?' she echoed. 'I don't think so.'

'Well, it doesn't call here again until Thursday, like I said.'

Rosa tried not to show how dismayed she felt. 'Oh, well, there's nothing I can do about it now. And Liam Jameson's the only lead I've got.'

Liam blew out a breath. 'Okay, okay. If that's your final word, I'll take you.'

'Take me where?'

'To Kilfoil Castle. That is where you want to go, isn't it?'

'Well, yes. But do you think Mr Jameson will agree to see me?'

'I'll make sure he does,' said Liam drily. 'Let's go.'

'But I don't even know who you are,' Rosa protested, the idea of getting into a car with a strange man suddenly assuming more importance than it had before.

'I'm—Luther Killian,' muttered Liam ungraciously, waiting for her to recognise the name of his main character. But there was no reaction. Her sister might read his books, but she definitely didn't.

CHAPTER THREE

ROSA hesitated. 'Um—is it far?' she ventured, drawing a sigh of impatience from the man beside her.

'Too far to walk, if that's what you're thinking,' he said shortly. 'There's always old McAllister, of course. He runs a part-time taxi service, if it's needed. I can't vouch for the reliability of his vehicle, though.'

Rosa glanced down at her bag which, even looped over her shoulder, was heavier than she'd expected when she'd packed it the previous day. 'Well, all right. Thanks,' she said, not without some misgivings. 'If it's not out of your way.'

Don't do me any favours, thought Liam irritably, reaching for her bag and opening the rear door of the car. He tossed it onto the seat and then gestured for her to get into the front. His leg was aching from standing too long and he couldn't wait to get off his feet.

'You didn't say if it was far,' she ventured, after he'd coiled his length behind the wheel, and Liam shrugged.

'The island's not that big,' he said, which wasn't really an answer. 'Don't worry. It won't take long to get there.'

Rosa hoped not, but the island did seem far bigger than she'd imagined as the Audi mounted the hill out of the village. They emerged onto a kind of plateau that stretched away ahead of them, very green and verdant, with small lakes, or lochs, glinting in the intermittent rays of the sun.

Away to their left, the mountains she'd seen from the quayside looked big and imposing. Their shadowy peaks were bathed in cloud cover, but the lower slopes changed from grey to purple where the native heather flourished among the rocks. Here and there the scrubland was dotted with trees, sturdy firs that could withstand the sudden shifts in the weather.

'This is Kilfoil Moor,' said her companion, nodding towards the open land at either side of the road. 'Don't be fooled by its look of substance. It's primitive bog in places. Even the sheep have more sense than to graze here.'

Rosa frowned. 'Are you a farmer, Mr Killian?'

A farmer! Liam felt a wry smile tug at his mouth. 'I own some land,' he agreed, neither admitting nor denying it. Then, to divert her, 'The island becomes much less hostile at the other side of the moor.'

'And have people—like—walked onto the moor and been swallowed up by the bog?' asked Rosa uneasily.

Liam cast her a mocking glance. 'Only in Jameson's books, I believe.'

Rosa grimaced. 'He sounds weird. I suppose living up here he can do virtually as he likes.'

'He's an author,' said Liam irritably, not appreciating her comments. 'For God's sake, he writes about monsters. That doesn't mean he *is* one!'

'I suppose.'

Rosa acknowledged that she was letting the isolation spook her. A curlew called, it wild cry sending a shiver down her spine. A covey of grouse, startled by the sound of the car, rose abruptly into the air, startling her. She made an incoherent sound and her companion turned to give her another curious look.

'Something wrong?'

Rosa shrugged. 'I was just thinking about what you said,' she replied, not altogether truthfully. 'I think I agree with you. Jameson wouldn't have brought Sophie here.'

'No?' Liam spoke guardedly.

'No. I mean—' She gestured towards the moor. 'I can't imagine any man who lives here going to somewhere frantic like a pop festival.' She paused. 'Can you?'

Liam's mouth compressed. 'I seem to remember saying much the same thing about half an hour ago,' he retorted.

'Oh. Oh, yes, you did.' Rosa pulled a face. 'I'm sorry. I think I should have listened to you.'

Liam shook his head. He didn't know what she expected him to say, what she expected him to do. But if she hoped that he'd turn the car around and drive her back to the village she was mistaken. He was tired, dammit. He'd just driven over five hundred miles, and there was no way she was going to add another twenty miles to his journey. If she wanted to go back, Sam would have to take her. Right now, he needed breakfast, a shower and his bed, not necessarily in that order.

Or that was what he told himself. In fact, he was curiously loath to abandon her. He felt sorry for her, he thought. She'd been sent up here on a wild goose chase and she was going to feel pretty aggrieved when she found out he'd been deceiving her, too.

The awareness of what he was thinking astounded him, however. This had always been his retreat, his sanctuary. The one place where he could escape the rat race of his life in London. What the hell was he doing, bringing a stranger into his home? For God's sake, *she* wasn't a teenager. She was plenty old enough to look out for herself.

'Anyway,' she said suddenly, 'I'm still going to ask him if he knows where she might be. I mean, if they are making a film up here, he will know about it. Where it's being made, I mean. Don't you think?'

Liam's fingers tightened on the wheel. Why didn't he just tell her who he was? he wondered impatiently. Why didn't he admit that he'd kept his identity a secret to begin with because he'd been half afraid she had some ulterior motive for coming here? She might not believe him, but it would be better than feeling a complete fraud every time she mentioned his name.

'Look, Miss—er—'

'Chantry,' she supplied equably. 'Rosa Chantry.'

'Yes. Miss Chantry.' Liam hesitated now. 'Look, I think there's something I—'

But before he could finish, she interrupted him. 'Oh, God!' she exclaimed in dismay, and for a moment he thought she'd realised who he was for herself. But then she reached into the back of the car, hauled her pack forward and extracted a mobile phone. 'I promised I'd ring my mother as soon as I reached the island,' she explained ruefully. 'Excuse me a minute. I've just got to tell her I'm all right before she begins to think she's lost two daughters instead of just one.'

'Yeah, but—' he began, about to tell her that there were no transmitters for cellphones on the island when she gave a frustrated cry.

'Dammit, the battery must be dead,' she exclaimed, looking at the instrument as if it was to blame for its inactivity. Then she frowned. 'That's funny. There's no signal at all.'

'That's because we don't have any mobile phone masts on Kilfoil,' said Liam mildly. 'The place was deserted for years—apart from a few hardy sheep—and although things have changed a bit since then, we prefer not to litter the island with all the detritus of the twenty-first century.'

'You mean I can't ring my mother?'

'No. There are landlines.'

'So do you think Liam Jameson will let me make a call from the castle?'

'I'm sure he will,' muttered Liam, aware he was retreating back into the character he'd created. 'Don't run away with the idea that the island's backwards. Since—since its modernisation, it's become quite a desirable place to live.'

Rosa arched brows that were several shades darker than her hair. 'Is that why you came here?' she asked. 'To escape the rat race?'

'In a manner of speaking.'

'And you like living here? You don't get—bored?'

'I'm never bored,' said Liam drily. 'Are you?'

'I don't get time to be bored,' she replied ruefully. 'I'm a schoolteacher. My work keeps me busy.'

'Ah.' Liam absorbed this. He thought it explained a lot. Like how she was able to come up here in the middle of August. Like why she seemed so prim and proper sometimes.

The moor was receding behind them now, and they'd started down a twisting road into the glen. He pointed ahead. 'There's the castle. What do you think?'

Rosa caught her breath. 'It's—beautiful,' she said, and it was. Standing square and solid on a headland overlooking the sea, its grey walls warmed by the strengthening sun, it was magnificent. 'It's very impressive,' she breathed.

And not what she had expected at all. 'But how can anyone live in such a place? It must have over a hundred rooms.'

'Fifty-three, actually,' said Liam unthinkingly. And then, with a grimace, 'Or so I've heard.'

'Fifty-three!' Rosa shook her head. 'He must be very rich.'

'Some of them are just anterooms,' said Liam, resenting the urge he had to defend himself, but doing it just the same. 'I'm fairly sure he doesn't use them all.'

'I should think not.' Rosa snorted. 'Is he married?'

'No.' Liam had no hesitation about telling her that. It was in the potted biography that appeared on the back of all his books, after all.

'Well, does he live alone?' Rosa was persistent. 'Does he have a girlfriend? Or a boyfriend?' she added, pulling a face. 'These days you never know.'

'He's not gay,' said Liam grimly. 'And he has household staff who run the place for him, so he's hardly alone.'

'All the same...' She was annoyingly resistant to his opinion. 'I bet he has to pay his employees well to get them to stay here.'

Liam clamped his jaws together and didn't answer her. He could have said that several of the people he employed were refugees from London, like himself. He did employ locals, where he could, but the islanders only wanted part-time work so they could pursue their own interests. The Highlanders were an independent lot and preferred fishing and farming to working indoors.

They approached the castle through open land dotted with sheep and cattle. Rosa saw shepherds' crofts nestling on the hillside, and more substantial farm buildings with whitewashed walls and smoking chimneys. A stream, which evidently had its source in the mountains, tumbled

over rocks on its way to the sea. And in the background
the shoreline beckoned, the sand clean and unblemished
and totally deserted.

Rosa knew that anyone who'd never seen this aspect of
Scotland wouldn't believe how incredibly beautiful it was.
The sea was calm here, and in places as green as—as
Luther Killian's eyes. And just as intriguing. Though
probably as cold as ice.

The castle itself looked just as splendid as they drew
closer. Although obviously renovations had been made,
they'd been accomplished in a way that didn't detract from
the building's charm and history. Only the square windows,
that had replaced the narrow lattices once used for firing
on the enemy in ancient times, were out of character. But
the heavy oak front doors looked just as solid a defence.

There were outbuildings set back from the main house,
with a cobbled forecourt edging the stone steps in front.
They approached over a wooden bridge spanning a dry
ditch, which might once have been a moat, and parked on
the forecourt to one side of the studded doors.

One of the doors opened immediately and a man and
several dogs stepped out into the sunlight. The dogs—two
golden retrievers and a spaniel—bounded down the steps
to greet them, their tails wagging excitedly.

To the accompaniment of their barks of welcome, Liam
swung open his door and hauled himself to his feet. Once
again, his leg had stiffened up and he cursed its weakness for
spoiling one of the true pleasures of his life. He had always
enjoyed driving and had a handful of expensive cars in his
possession. He preferred them to the helicopter that his agent
had insisted was essential, and leased the aircraft to the local
air ambulance service more often than he used it himself.

Steeling himself against the pain, he left the car and strode towards Sam Devlin, the man who ran Kilfoil for him with such consummate skill and efficiency. 'Liam—' began Sam, only to break off when his employer raised a warning finger to his lips. 'It's good to see you again,' he amended, his grey brows drawing together in confusion. 'Is something wrong?'

Liam glanced back significantly, and now Sam saw Rosa getting out of the car. 'Do we have a visitor?' he asked in surprise. He knew, better than anyone, that Liam never brought strangers to Kilfoil.

'We do,' said Liam in a low voice, after shaking hands with the older man. 'She's here because she wants to ask *Liam Jameson* where her sister is.'

'What?' Sam stared at him. 'But you're—'

'She doesn't know that.' Liam sighed. 'It's long story, Sam, but now's not the time to share it. Just play along, will you? I intend to tell her who I am, but—not yet.'

Sam grimaced. 'But why bring her here—?' he began, and then broke off when the young woman left the car and started towards them. She was slowed by the snuffling of the dogs, but she was too near now for them to continue their conversation. He collected himself with an effort. 'Welcome to Kilfoil, miss.'

'This is Sam Devlin, Liam Jameson's second-in-command,' said Liam smoothly. 'Sam, this is Miss Chantry. Rosa Chantry, isn't that right?' He looked to her for confirmation. 'Perhaps Mrs Wilson would be kind enough to provide Miss Chantry with lunch.'

'I'm sure she'd try,' Sam agreed drily, but Rosa couldn't impose on her host in that way.

'Actually,' she said, 'if I could just have a quick word with Mr Jameson—?'

'Mr Jameson's—tied up at present, Miss Chantry,' said Sam, with a wry look at his employer. 'If you'll come with me, I'll show you where you can wait.'

'Oh, but—do you think he will see me?'

Rosa addressed her words to Sam now, even though Liam had assured her he'd arrange it himself.

Sam looked at his employer blankly. 'I think it's—possible,' he said, gaining a nod of approval. 'Um—why don't you follow me?'

Rosa hesitated, turning to the man who'd driven her here with a grateful smile. 'Thanks for the lift,' she said. 'Goodbye, Mr Killian.'

Liam inclined his head, aware that Sam was staring at him, open-mouthed. 'My pleasure,' he replied, realising he meant it. He turned away as Sam pulled himself together and led her into the castle. She wasn't going to be so pleased when she discovered who he really was.

Meanwhile, Rosa was experiencing an unwarranted feeling of regret that she wouldn't be seeing Luther Killian again. He had been kind, in spite of her ingratitude. She wished she'd asked him where he lived now. After all, whatever happened later, she was going to be stuck on the island for at least another couple of days.

She followed Liam Jameson's man into the castle with some reluctance. Despite her desire to speak to Jameson and get this over with, it was a little daunting being faced with such surroundings. Although the hall they entered via an anteroom was brightly lit by several wall sconces, and the huge fire that was burning in the grate, it was intimidating. With its lofty ceiling and tapestry-hung walls, it reminded her that the man she'd come to see made his living from scaring his readers.

'We only use the hall as a reception room,' Sam Devlin offered, as she hovered just inside the door. 'The rest of the castle is much more cosy. It would be impossible to keep the place warm otherwise.'

Rosa could believe it. 'Does Mr Jameson live here all the year round?'

Sam seemed to consider his words before replying. 'Mostly,' he said at last. 'Except when he's away on business or pleasure. Now, please come this way.'

To Rosa's surprise, and trepidation, they crossed the hall to where a winding flight of stone stairs led to an upper floor. Although the stairs were carpeted, Rosa viewed them without enthusiasm. She'd assumed the man was going to show her into one of the rooms that opened off the hall.

'Wouldn't it be easier if I just waited here for Mr Jameson?' she asked.

'I'm afraid not.' Sam was polite, but resolute. 'This floor of the castle is given over to kitchens and storerooms, as well as providing living quarters for the full-time staff.'

'I see.' Rosa was reassured by the idea that there were other people living as well as working here. Luther Killian hadn't told her that.

With no alternative, she followed the man up the stairs, realising as she did so that this must be one of the towers she'd seen from the road. She wasn't good with spiral staircases, but happily it opened out onto a narrow landing, with windows in an outer wall that gave an uninterrupted view of the bay.

'Oh, isn't that wonderful!' she exclaimed, pausing at a window embrasure and gazing out at the view. The windows overlooked the front of the castle, with the little bridge they'd driven over just below her. And she saw, with some surprise, that Luther Killian's car was still parked in the same spot. Frowning, she glanced round at Sam Devlin. 'Um—Mr Killian's still here.'

'Is he?' Sam didn't sound particularly interested, and then Rosa remembered Killian had said he'd speak to Liam Jameson himself. He might be explaining the situation. If so, that would be something else she had to thank him for. Maybe she'd ask Sam Devlin where Killian lived before she left.

But thinking about leaving reminded her that she still hadn't phoned her mother. 'Er—do you think I could make a phone call while I'm waiting?' she ventured, and Sam shrugged.

'There's a phone in here,' he said, opening a door into what appeared to be a library. 'Make yourself at home. I'll ask Mrs Wilson to provide some refreshments.'

'You will tell Mr Jameson I'm here?' Rosa reminded him, wondering about the rather curious look that crossed his face at her words.

'I'll tell him,' he agreed, remaining on the landing. 'If you'll excuse me...?'

Rosa nodded, trying not to feel apprehensive when he closed the door rather firmly behind him. Well, she was here. She'd reached her destination. And if the circumstances were not what she'd expected, it wasn't her fault.

Turning, she surveyed the room with determined confidence. One wall curved, as if it was part of the tower she'd just climbed, but all the walls were lined with bookshelves. There was a granite-topped desk, strewn with papers and a laptop computer, and several leather chairs.

Rosa wondered if these were Liam Jameson's books, but there were obviously too many for that to be so. Approaching one of the shelves, she drew out a bulky tome, hand-carved in leather. But the title, *Vampire Myths of the Fifteenth Century*, made her hastily push it back again.

But she was wasting time, she thought, noticing the neat black instrument set at one end of the desk. She had to call her mother. Mrs Chantry would probably be biting her nails by this time. Particularly if she'd tried to ring Rosa herself.

As she waited for the connection, Rosa perched on the edge of the window seat. The walls were thick and the sills were broad, plenty broad enough to provide a comfortable seat. Glancing down, she saw that from this angle she could see the gardens at the back of the castle, and a couple of huge glasshouses, set into the lee of the tower.

Obviously the place was self-sufficient, she thought. And, despite her initial reaction, Rosa quite envied Jameson for living here. It was peaceful in a way very few places were these days.

Then, her mother answered. 'Rosa? Rosa, is that you? Have you found Sophie? Is she all right?'

'I haven't found her.' Rosa decided there was no point in prevaricating. 'There isn't a film crew on the island, Mum. Sophie must have been making it up.'

'Oh, she wouldn't do that.' Mrs Chantry was so gullible where her younger daughter was concerned. 'If she's not there, then Mark must have made a mistake. Scotland's a big place. They must be filming somewhere else.'

'But where?'

'I don't know, do I? That's for you to find out.'

'Perhaps.' Rosa was non-committal. 'I may know more after I've spoken to Liam Jameson himself.'

'You mean you haven't spoken to him personally?'

'How could I?'

'Well, for heaven's sake, Rosa, what have you been doing?'

'Getting here,' retorted Rosa indignantly. 'It was a long journey, you know.'

'So where are you now? Sitting in some bar in Mallaig, I suppose. And who told you there's no film being made on the island?'

'As a matter of fact, I'm on the island at this moment. I'm at Kilfoil Castle. And I'm pretty sure that nothing's going on here.'

Her mother snorted. 'So if Jameson's not there—'

'I didn't say that,' Rosa interrupted. 'Haven't I just said I'll know more after I've spoken to him?'

'So he's not with the production?'

If he ever was. 'It would appear not,' said Rosa trying to be patient. She heard the sound of someone opening the library door. 'Look, I've got to go, Mum. I'll ring you later. As soon as I have some news.'

She rang off before Mrs Chantry could issue any more instructions. Then, getting up from the window seat, she turned to find Luther Killian standing just inside the door. He'd evidently changed. The crumpled shirt and jeans he'd worn to travel in had been replaced by a long-sleeved purple knit shirt and drawstring cotton trousers. Judging by the drops of water sparkling on his dark hair, he'd had a shower as well.

Rosa knew her jaw had dropped, and she quickly rescued it. 'Oh, hi,' she said, a little nonplussed. 'I thought you'd gone.'

Well, she'd thought he would have by now.

Liam's smile was guarded. 'Is everything all right at

home?' he asked, guessing what had been going on. He pushed the tips of his fingers into the back pockets of his pants. 'You look—surprised to see me.'

'I am.' Rosa didn't think there was any point in lying about it. 'Have you spoken to Liam Jameson? Has he agreed to see me?'

'He has,' said Liam drily, finding this harder than he'd expected. 'I'm sorry to disappoint you, Rosa, but I'm Liam Jameson.'

Rosa stared at him aghast. 'You're kidding!'

'No.' Liam pulled a face, and then, abandoning his awkward stance, he crossed to the desk and went to stand behind it. 'I didn't intend to deceive you. Not initially. It just worked out that way.'

CHAPTER FOUR

'YOU'RE NOT SERIOUSLY going to allow her to stay here until she can get a ferry back to the mainland, are you?' Sam Devlin was dismayed. 'Man, you know nothing about this woman. How do you know this wasn't just a ruse to get into the castle?'

'I don't.' Liam finished the plate of bacon and eggs Mrs Wilson had cooked for him and reached for his steaming mug of coffee, sitting on the gleaming pine table beside him. He took a mouthful of the coffee, the third cup he'd had that morning, and sighed his satisfaction. 'But, in answer to your first question, she's leaving this morning. As soon as she can get her belongings packed.'

'Well, that's a mercy,' said Sam briskly. 'I could hardly believe it when Edith told me she was staying the night. Not but what the lassie seems honest enough. It's just unlike you to invite a stranger into your home.'

'I know.' Liam could hear the edge in his voice, but he didn't appreciate Sam telling him what he already knew. 'Anyway, I doubt if you'd have wanted to drive her back to the village last night.'

Sam sniffed. 'You could always have called McAllister out. He gets little enough work as it is.'

'Well, I didn't,' said Liam shortly. 'And, for your information, I don't think she has an ulterior motive for being here. For God's sake, she didn't know who I was until I told her.'

'So you say.'

'So I know.'

'All right, all right.' Sam backed down. 'But I'm always suspicious when supposedly innocent strangers turn up out of the blue. I mean, who would be stupid enough as to believe you'd allow anyone to make a film on Kilfoil?'

'Her teenage sister, perhaps?'

'But you have nothing to do with film production.'

'I told her that,' said Liam mildly.

'So why did you bring her here? Couldn't you have convinced her you were telling the truth and sent her on her way?'

'She wanted to come,' said Liam flatly. 'She insisted on speaking to Liam Jameson in person.'

Sam shook his head. 'This was when you were masquerading as Luther Killian?'

'If you want to put it that way, yes.'

Sam snorted. 'Well, I don't know what you were thinking of, Liam. For God's sake, you're not a teenager. You're a middle-aged writer of horror fiction. You should have known better.'

'Gee, it's so good to know what you think of me,' drawled Liam drily. 'Why didn't you add with more scars than Ben Nevis and a gammy leg into the bargain?'

Sam's gnarled cheeks had gained a little colour now. 'Och, you know what I think of you, man. Surely there's no need for me to mince my words.' He paused, and when his employer didn't say anything he continued fiercely, 'If you were the type who played around with the lassies, Liam, it would be different. But you're not. You never have been. Sure, I know you've had the odd fling now and then, but you've never brought your conquests home. Not since Kayla—'

'Don't go there, Sam.'

Liam came to life now, and the older man hunched his shoulders at the reproof. It was years since he'd even thought about Kayla Stevens, thought Liam grimly. The woman he'd been intending to marry before the disastrous attack that had almost killed him.

They'd met at a launch party his publisher had thrown for him when his first book had made number one on the bestseller lists. Kayla had been a struggling model, hired out by her agent for such occasions to add a little glamour to the mix. She'd seemed out of place there, too innocent to be forced to earn a living in that way. Liam had felt sorry for her—much as he'd done for Rosa Chantry, he thought now, scowling at the memory. But he'd eventually learned that Kayla had always had an eye to the main chance.

Although she'd hung around the hospital for a while after the attack, the idea of getting hitched to a man who was badly scarred, who might be impotent or paralysed, and who would definitely need a lot of care and understanding to recover, hadn't appealed to Kayla. Six months after returning Liam's ring, she'd married a South American polo player with enough money to keep her in the style to which she'd become accustomed. The fact that without Liam she'd never have had the opportunity to meet such a man didn't even compute.

Sam was looking dejected now, and Liam took pity on him. 'Look, this isn't about what Kayla did, right? It's about helping someone out. Rosa's mother doesn't know where her younger daughter is. I expect she's pretty worried by now.'

'So why doesn't she go to the police?'

'And say what? That her daughter's gone off with another man and her boyfriend's jealous? Sam, teenagers are notoriously unpredictable. She'll probably turn up in a couple of days and deny the whole thing.'

'So why did you get involved?'

Good question. 'I've been asking myself that,' admitted Liam sagely. 'I don't know. Because my name was mentioned, I suppose. According to Rosa, her sister's a big fan. Maybe I was flattered. In any case, she's leaving today.'

It was the sunlight that awakened her. When she'd finally gone to bed—some time after midnight, she thought— she'd been sure she wouldn't sleep and the moonlight had been comforting. But she must have been more tired than she'd thought, both mentally and physically. Otherwise, why would she have accepted that man's help?

Discovering that the man she knew as Luther Killian was really Liam Jameson had knocked her off balance. And angered her, too, she admitted. He'd had no right to lie about his identity, however desperate he was to retain his anonymity.

The fact that he must have been equally stunned to learn that he was supposed to have met her sister at a pop festival and offered her a screen test made it marginally excusable. But she wouldn't have come here at all if he'd been honest with her from the start.

Pushing back the duvet, Rosa swung her legs out of bed and padded, barefoot, to the windows. The floor was cold beneath her feet, but she thought she'd never get tired of the view. She was on the second floor of the castle and her windows looked out over the headland. She had an uninterrupted view of the restless sea that broke against the rocks.

It was so beautiful, the sun already tingeing the tips of the waves with gold. But there were clouds on the horizon, brooding things which threatened rain later. Perhaps this afternoon, she considered, wondering where she'd be sleeping tonight.

The realisation that it must be later than she'd thought occurred belatedly. Or perhaps it was the appetising aroma of warm bread drifting to her nostrils that reminded her she hadn't eaten much the night before. She turned with a start to find there was a tray resting on the chest of drawers standing by the doorway. Someone had evidently put it there. Was that what had woken her?

She'd been resting her bare knee on the wide sill, but now she straightened and headed back to the bed, where she'd left her watch. Snatching it up from the nightstand, she saw it was already half-past-nine. Good heavens, she must have slept for at least eight hours.

She hesitated, torn between getting washed and dressed or investigating the contents of the tray. The tray won out, and, deciding that whoever had put it there deserved to be compensated, she picked it up and carried it back to the window seat.

A flask of what was obviously coffee invited her to try it. There was milk and cream in small jugs, brown sugar, and a basket of warm rolls. These were what she'd smelled, she realised, touching them reverently. Warm rolls, giving off the delicious scents of raisin and cinnamon.

Had Liam Jameson arranged this for her? More likely

Mrs Wilson, she thought, remembering how rude she'd been to her host the afternoon before. But learning that he had been Liam Jameson all along had been so humiliating. When he'd told her he was the man she'd been waiting to see, she'd felt hopelessly out of her depth...

'You?' she'd said stupidly. '*You're* Liam Jameson?' She shook her head. 'You can't be.'

He was annoyingly laconic. 'Why not?'

'Because you don't look anything like your picture,' Rosa protested, remembering the young man with a moustache and goatee beard she'd seen on the back cover of one of his novels. This man's face was clean-shaven, if you didn't count the shadow of stubble on his chin.

'Well, I'm sorry to disappoint you, but I really am Liam Jameson,' he said. 'The picture I think you're referring to was taken about twelve years ago.'

'Then you ought to have it updated,' she snapped.

As if!

Liam shrugged. 'As I believe I told you earlier, I'm a fairly reclusive soul. I prefer not to be recognised.'

'That's no excuse.' Rosa was trying hard not to feel too let down. 'So, what about Sophie? Do you know where she is?'

'Of course not.' The exasperation in his voice was unmistakable. 'If I did, don't you think I'd have told you?'

'I don't know what to think, do I?' Rosa's nails dug into her palms. 'You bring me here under false pretences...'

'Now, wait a minute.' Liam didn't know why her words stung him so much. That *was*, in effect, what he'd done. Taking a different tack, he went on, 'Would you have believed me if I'd told you who I was? You've just accused me of not looking anything like my picture.' He paused. 'If you must know, I felt sorry for you. You'd obviously been sent on a wasted journey, and whatever I'd said you would still have been stuck here for three more days.'

Rosa lifted her chin at this. 'There was no need for you to feel sorry for me, Mr Jameson.'

'Wasn't there?' Liam couldn't help but admire her courage. He'd obviously judged her too harshly when he'd thought she had no spirit. 'So—what? If I'd told you who I was, you'd have just booked into a bed and breakfast and waited for Thursday's ferry? You wouldn't have been at all suspicious that I might not have been telling you the truth?'

'Well, I would have asked you about Sophie,' said Rosa, her shoulders slumping. 'You should have told me who you were,' she added again. 'Who is Luther Killian anyway? Someone who works for you?'

'You might say that.' A trace of humour crossed his face, and she was annoyed to feel herself responding to his charm. 'Luther Killian is the main character in all my novels. Which just proves that you're not a fan.'

'I've told you, Sophie is the one who reads your books.' She shook her head bitterly. 'You must think I'm such a fool.'

'Why would I think that?'

He had the nerve to look indignant, but Rosa was way past being understanding. 'Because I was too stupid to suspect anything,' she retorted. 'Even when it became obvious that you knew too much about him not to be involved.' She took a deep breath. 'Why did you do it, Mr Jameson? Were you just playing a game? Did making a fool of me turn you on?'

Now, where had that come from?

Rosa was still gazing at him, horrified at what she'd said, when someone knocked at the door. There was a moment when she feared Liam Jameson was going to ignore it, but then he turned and strode across the room. Once more, he was dragging his leg, but Rosa was too dismayed to feel any compassion for him. God in heaven, he would think she was no better than her sister.

The housekeeper was waiting outside. She was carrying a tray of tea and sandwiches, and Liam let her into the room with controlled politeness.

'This is Mrs Wilson,' he said, his voice as cold as she'd heard it. 'Enjoy your lunch. I'll speak to you later.'

But in fact he hadn't. When Mrs Wilson had come in to collect the tray again, she'd offered the news that Mr Jameson was resting. He'd apparently asked the housekeeper to provide a room for her, where she could freshen up and so on. And that was how Rosa came to be here, almost twenty-four hours after her arrival.

Not that she'd ever expected to stay the night. When she'd had as much of the tea and sandwiches as she could stomach, with her conscience making every mouthful an effort, she'd ventured downstairs with the tray, hoping to run into her host. But the only person she'd encountered was Sam Devlin, and he'd taken some pleasure in telling her that Mr Jameson was indisposed and wouldn't be able to speak to her that afternoon after all.

Naturally, Rosa had blamed herself for Jameson's condition, sure that her behaviour had contributed to his malaise. But when she'd asked how she could get back to the village, Devlin had reluctantly admitted that his employer didn't want her to leave until he'd spoken to her again.

'Mr Jameson suggests that you might like to spend a little time exploring the grounds of the castle,' he'd said tersely. 'I can come with you, if you like? Or, if not, you're free to relax in the library. There are plenty of books to read, and Mrs Wilson can supply anything else you need.'

In the event, Rosa had agreed to go for a walk, though not with Sam Devlin. She'd a managed to convince the dour Scotsman that she wouldn't get lost, and she'd spent a fairly pleasant hour wandering through gardens bright with late summer flowers, with only the dogs for company.

Back at the castle, and not knowing what else to do, she'd retreated to the library. Though not to read. She'd seen what manner of books were on the shelves, and, while she was sure Jameson only used them for research, she'd had no desire to give herself nightmares.

She'd been a little disturbed when Mrs Wilson had informed her that supper would be served at seven in the dining hall. She'd never expected to stay for supper and she hadn't been wholly surprised when she'd ventured downstairs again, after washing her face and combing her hair, to find that she was eating alone.

'Mr Jameson has suggested you spend the night,' Mrs Wilson had explained gently, much less antagonistic than Sam Devlin had been. 'He says he'll see you in the morning. Will that be all right?'

Of course Rosa knew she should have refused, that accepting anything from Liam Jameson was putting herself in his debt. Which was definitely something she didn't want to do. But she also knew that she owed him an apology, and much against her better judgment she'd agreed to stay.

She sighed now. Whether she'd wanted to or not, she'd accepted his hospitality, and sooner or later she was going to have to make her apologies and take her leave. So, was her reluctance just embarrassment, or was she, as she suspected, curiously unwilling to say goodbye?

She shivered. How ridiculous was that? Liam Jameson meant nothing to her, and she'd made sure he would be glad to see the back of her. And what a way to repay his kindness. Okay, he should have told her who he was right off—but would she have believed him as he'd said?

She considered. On the ferry, she'd told him very little about why she was coming to the island, and even after they'd disembarked she hadn't exactly welcomed his help. By the time she'd confessed why she was really here, he'd already let her think he only knew Liam Jameson, not that that was who he really was.

The situation had definitely not been conducive to confidences, and she had to admit she'd been too anxious to get to her destination to listen to reason. Was that really why he'd kept his identity from her, as he'd said? It certainly made more sense than what she'd accused him of.

Not wanting to think about that scene in the library, Rosa finished her coffee and one of the warm rolls, and then went to get a shower. A glimpse of her tumbled hair convinced her that she couldn't face Jameson in her present condition. She needed to have herself firmly under control before she encountered him again.

The bathroom was just as elegant as the bedroom where she'd slept, with a free-standing claw-footed tub and mirrored walls. The fluted glass shower could have accommodated at least three occupants, and the windows were made of clear glass.

The idea that anyone could look into the bathroom as she had her shower sent Rosa immediately to the windows. But there, on the second floor of the castle, there was no danger of being observed by anyone. Open spaces stretched in all directions, the nearest dwelling at least a mile away.

Stripping off the man-sized tee shirt she'd brought to sleep in, Rosa was caught for a moment by her reflection in the mirrored walls. Long legs, small breasts and a bony frame did not make for beauty, she decided ruefully. Okay, her complexion was fair, her eyes were dark and she didn't suffer from freckles. But her mouth was too wide, her nose was too long and at present there were frown lines between her brows.

She sighed, losing patience with herself and stepping into the shower. What did it matter what she looked like? Liam Jameson was not going to be attracted to her. Goodness, she'd thought he was gorgeous when she'd believed he was Luther Killian. Now she knew who he really was, she would not have been surprised if Sophie had fallen for him.

Sophie!

Rosa felt ashamed of herself. Here she was, thinking about Liam Jameson, when she still had no idea where her sister was. She would have to phone her mother again, she thought, knowing Mrs Chantry would be waiting for her call. Hopefully her mother would realise that Rosa wasn't free to use Liam Jameson's phone at random. Particularly when the call she needed to make was long distance.

Emerging from the shower a few moments later, she quickly grabbed one of the luxury towels from the rack and wrapped it about her. Then, after cleaning her teeth, she went back into the bedroom to dress.

To her surprise, and dismay, the tray had disappeared in her absence. Remembering that she hadn't bothered closing the bathroom door, Rosa hoped she hadn't been seen. But if she had it would only have been Mrs Wilson, she assured herself. There was no way Liam Jameson would have collected the tray himself.

And if he had, what of it? she asked herself bitterly. It wasn't as if she was the kind of woman men spied on. Unlike Sophie, who, with her spiky hair and rounded figure, was always being pursued by one man or another. And it now seemed as if her involvement with Mark Campion was on the skids as well.

Thankfully, there was a hairdryer lying on the period dressing table in the bedroom. Like the bathroom, the bedroom was an attractive mix of ancient and modern. The cheval mirror was Victorian, and the chest of drawers was even older. But, although the bed was a four-poster, the mattress was reassuringly twenty-first century in design.

It took a little while to dry her mass of hair, and then even more time to secure it in a French braid. If the severe style and the high-necked navy sweater she chose to wear with her jeans owed anything to a desire to stifle any trace of femininity, she refused to acknowledge it. It was important to appear confident, however insecure she might feel.

She was quite familiar with the stairs that led down to the lower floor by this time. The dining hall was on the floor below, not far from the library. But the dining hall, with its mahogany-lined walls and long refectory table, was empty, the epergne of roses in the centre the only sign of life.

She wondered if it was worth going down into the reception hall, but she doubted she'd encounter her host there. If, indeed, he was up and about. But she remembered there had been a desk and a computer in the library. Perhaps that was where Jameson wrote his books.

She tapped at the library door first, before venturing inside. But, although she listened intently for any movement from within, the room seemed eerily quiet. Now, why had she used that adjective? she chided herself. She hadn't felt any unusual presence in the castle. It was just her imagination working overtime because there was nobody about.

There was only one way to find out. Reaching for the handle, she turned the knob. She sensed she wasn't alone only seconds before someone spoke behind her. 'Looking for me?' enquired Liam Jameson in a hollow voice, and she almost jumped out of her skin.

CHAPTER FIVE

'I—YES. YES,' she said, dry-mouthed, her breathing quickening uncontrollably. She swung round to find him propped against the wall to one side of the heavy door. Then, seeing his mocking smile, she forgot all about the promises she'd made herself. 'Did you do that on purpose?' she demanded hotly.

'Do what?' Liam adopted an innocent expression, but he could tell from her face that she knew he had.

'Try to frighten me,' she exclaimed, pressing a hand to her chest, where her heart was beating wildly. 'Honestly—' she endeavoured to calm herself '—you almost gave me a heart attack.'

'I'm sorry.'

But he didn't sound particularly sorry, and Rosa recoiled instinctively when he leant past her and pushed open the door. 'After you,' he said, apparently unaware that his hand had brushed the side of her breast as he did so. Her breast tingled, and Rosa stiffened, but he seemed indifferent to her response.

However, Liam wasn't indifferent, and he was glad when she turned and went ahead of him into the room. For God's sake, he thought, annoyed with himself as much as her. She was behaving like an outraged virgin and he was experiencing the kind of reaction that would have been pathetic when he was a teenager.

What was wrong with him, for pity's sake? He had no interest in repressed spinsters. Women who knew little about sex, and what they did know scared them rigid. When he needed a woman, he preferred one who knew the score.

All the same, a little voice inside him taunted, it might be amusing to see how she'd react if he came on to her. It was years since he'd used sex as anything more than an infrequent necessity, with good reason. And just because Rosa Chantry intrigued him, it was no reason to think anything had changed. She'd be just as horrified as Kayla had been when she'd seen his injuries. But it would have been so nice to pull the pins out of her hair and feel all that fiery silk spilling into his hands...

Once again he steeled himself against that kind of madness. Despite the ache between his legs, he was determined not to give her another reason to accuse him of upsetting her. Hell, he didn't need that kind of aggravation, but if that childish plait and masculine outfit were intended to deter any thoughts of a sexual nature they were having quite the opposite effect.

He closed the door behind him, leaning back against it, struggling to gain control of his sudden need. Rosa had hurried across the room, meanwhile, obviously wanting to put a safe distance between them. Then, when she felt she'd achieved her objective, she turned to face him.

'I—*was* looking for you,' she said, linking her hands together at her waist, unaware that it was a particularly protective stance. 'I wanted to thank you.'

'To thank me?' Liam couldn't think of anything she'd want to thank him for, but Rosa's lips had tightened.

'For allowing me to stay the night,' she informed him primly. 'You didn't have to do that.'

'Ah.' Liam was relieved to feel the restriction in his trousers easing, and he straightened away from the door. 'No problem.' He waited a beat. 'Were you comfortable?'

'Very comfortable, thank you.'

'Good.' Liam came further into the room. 'I'm sorry I had to leave you on your own all evening. I'm afraid I fell asleep, and didn't wake until after midnight.'

Rosa was tempted to say, *How appropriate* bearing in mind his occupation, but she didn't. She was still intensely aware of him, and inviting that kind of intimacy wasn't sensible. 'It's all right,' she said instead. 'Your housekeeper looked after me. I slept really well.'

'You weren't afraid I might turn into a vampire in the night and ravish you?' Liam couldn't resist the urge to tease her and she flushed.

'Only briefly,' she retorted, surprising him again. 'But I'm fairly sure vampires don't ride ferries or drive cars in broad daylight.'

'Luther Killian does,' he said at once, and Rosa gave him an old-fashioned look.

'Luther Killian doesn't exist,' she said. 'Or only in your imagination, anyway.'

'You think?'

Rosa shook her head. 'You're not telling me you believe in vampires, Mr Jameson?'

'Oh, yes.' He nodded. 'There have been too many reports of sightings, both here and in Eastern Europe. And if you went to New Orleans—'

'Which I'm not likely to do,' she said tightly, realising she was letting him distract her from her purpose. She ought to be asking him if she could use his phone again, instead of indulging in a discussion about mythical monsters. Shrugging, she made a face. 'I know very little about such things, Mr Jameson. But I imagine it makes good publicity for your books.'

Liam caught his breath. 'You think that's all it is?' He was indignant.

'Well, I don't know, do I? I know nothing about vampires.'

'You know they don't normally go out in sunlight,' he reminded her, and she sighed.

'Everyone knows that.' And then, unable to resist it, 'Except Luther Killian, apparently.'

'Ah, but Luther is only *half* inhuman. His mother was a witch before she met Luther's dad.'

Rosa couldn't help smiling. 'And he converted her, I suppose?'

'Vampires always convert their victims,' agreed Liam, closing the space between them. 'D'you want me to show you how?'

Rosa backed up. 'I know how, Mr Jameson,' she mumbled, not sure if he was teasing her now or not. 'Please—' She held out her hand in front of her. 'I'm not a character in one of your books.'

'No,' he conceded flatly, aware that he was in danger of allowing their relationship to develop into something it was not. He turned back towards his desk, hearing her sudden relieved intake of breath as he did so. 'You're obviously not a believer.'

Rosa sighed now. She didn't want to offend him, for

heaven's sake. 'A believer in what?' she asked, much against her better judgement, and he turned to rest his hips against the granite surface.

'In the supernatural,' he said carelessly, folding his arms. 'What was it you said on the way here? Ghosts and were-wolves—we call them shapechangers, by the way—and things that go bump in the night.'

Rosa shrugged. 'And you are?'

'Oh, sure. Anyone who has encountered evil in its purest form has to be.'

Rosa frowned. 'Are you saying *you've* encountered evil?'

Oh, yes.

For a moment Liam thought he'd said the words out loud, but the expectant look on her face assured him he hadn't. Thank God!

'I suppose we all encounter evil in one form or another,' he prevaricated, having no intention of discussing his experiences with her. He'd already stepped too far over the mark, and he backtracked into the only avenue open to him. 'Luther certainly has.'

'Oh, Luther!' She was disparaging. 'Who's only a character in your books.'

'The main character,' he corrected her. 'He's what you'd call an anti-hero. He kills, but his intentions are always good.'

'Isn't that a contradiction in terms?' she exclaimed at once. 'How can anyone—or anything—that makes a living killing people be regarded as good?'

Liam shrugged, and as he did so Rosa caught a glimpse of something silvery against his neck. It was either a birthmark or a scar of some sort, and her mouth went dry. It occurred to her that it might have been made by someone's—or something's—teeth.

Oh, God!

'I suppose that depends on your definition of good and evil,' he replied, diverting her. 'Isn't ridding the world of genuinely wicked individuals worthy of some respect?'

Rosa struggled to regain her objectivity. 'And that's what your books are about? Some—some vampire bounty-hunter working to make the world a better place?'

'A safer place, anyway,' agreed Liam drily. 'Don't knock it. You never know what you'd do if you were faced with primal evil.'

'And you do?' She sounded sceptical, and Liam had to bite his tongue not to tell her exactly what had happened to him. 'Come on, Mr Jameson. We both know you've lived a charmed life.'

Liam had to tuck his fingers beneath his arms to prevent himself from tearing his clothes aside to show her the kind of evil he'd encountered. 'Maybe,' he managed tersely. 'But I haven't always lived in Scotland, Miss Chantry.'

'I know.' She'd relaxed a little now. 'I read about you on the Internet. Didn't you used to work at the Stock Exchange, or somewhere?'

'It was a merchant bank, actually.'

'Whatever.' Rosa shrugged, glad of the return to reality. 'I imagine you had a fairly good salary. Then you made a lot of money with your first book and bought your own castle. How difficult was that?'

Liam pushed himself to his feet. 'If that's what you want to think,' he said, turning to shuffle the papers on his desk. 'Which reminds me, I have work to do.'

Rosa felt ashamed now. It wasn't anything to do with her how he lived his life. 'Look,' she said, taking a step towards him, 'I'll admit I know nothing about you, really.

And—and if you say you know how it feels to face real evil, then I believe you. But—'

'But you don't believe me,' said Liam sharply, swinging around again, and Rosa was uneasily aware that there was barely a hand's breadth between them now. 'You're humouring me, Miss Chantry, and I don't like it. I don't need your endorsement.'

Rosa licked her dry lips. 'I was only being polite,' she protested. 'It's not my fault if you're touchy about the veracity of your books.'

'Touchy about the veracity—' Liam gazed at her angrily. 'You haven't the first idea what you're talking about.' He dragged a calming breath into his lungs and tried to speak naturally. 'Let's just say I have had some firsthand knowledge of evil. But I'd rather not discuss it. Okay?'

Rosa lifted her shoulders. 'I had no idea.'

'Why should you?' Liam wasn't at all sure he liked the look of sympathy in her eyes any better than the disbelief he'd seen before. 'Forget it. I have.'

Though he doubted he ever would.

Rosa hesitated. 'I didn't mean to suggest your books weren't believable,' she persisted, laying a reckless hand on his sleeve. 'I'm sorry if I've offended you.'

Offended me?

Liam expelled a strangled breath. Although he was wearing a warm sweatshirt, he could feel the touch of her fingers clear through to his skin. The muscles in his arm tightened almost instinctively, the tendons heating and expanding much like those other muscles between his legs.

'It's not important,' he muttered harshly, concentrating on anything but the feminine scent of her skin. But

then he lifted his lids and encountered those anxious
brown eyes, and he felt as if he was drowning in their soft
depths.

Hardly aware of what he was doing, he lifted his hand
and brushed his thumb across her parted lips. Moisture that
had gathered there clung to the pad, and he didn't think
before bringing his thumb to his mouth to taste her.

For her part, Rosa was almost paralysed by his actions.
She'd never dreamt that an innocent attempt to comfort him
might have such a disturbing result. Her whole body felt
hot and trembly now, and she was aware of him in a way
that she hadn't been before. Or was she only kidding
herself? She'd been aware of him right from the start.

When her tongue emerged to circle her lips it was
because they'd suddenly gone dry, not to absorb any lin-
gering trace of his scent. Although she did. She heard him
suck in a breath and wondered what he was thinking. Dear
God, this wasn't meant to happen. But she knew that Colin
had never made her feel anything like this.

When he spoke, however, his tone was harsh. 'I
shouldn't have done that,' he said shortly. 'I'm sorry.'

Now it was Rosa's turn to take a gulp of much-needed
oxygen. 'It—doesn't matter,' she said, glancing behind
him at the telephone. 'Um—' She had to calm down, she
told herself. 'I was wondering if—'

But that was as far as she got. 'It does matter,' he said,
raking back his dark hair with a frustrated hand. 'For God's
sake, you must think I'm desperate for a woman!'

Liam saw the way his words affected her almost before
he'd finished speaking. The fact that he'd been trying to
reassure himself that his emotions weren't involved here
was no excuse. He realised, belatedly, that what he'd said

could be taken two ways, and he wasn't at all surprised when she turned on him.

'I'm sure you're not,' she retorted stiffly, wrapping her arms tightly across her slim body so that her small breasts were pushed upward in an unknowingly provocative way. 'And I'm not that desperate for a man, either.'

Liam suppressed a groan. Didn't she realise he hadn't intended to offend her? Evidently not. He scowled. Now it was up to him to defuse the situation he'd created, and one look at her face convinced him that it wouldn't be easy.

'Look,' he said persuasively, 'that wasn't intended as an insult. On the contrary. I wouldn't like you to think I expected any payment for my hospitality, that's all.'

Rosa gave him a disbelieving look. 'We both know what you meant, Mr Jameson,' she said tightly. 'I'm not a fool. You don't have to tell me I'm not the type of woman someone like you would find appealing.'

Liam felt a twinge of indignation. Despite the warning voice of his conscience, which was telling him not to continue with this, he resented the contempt he'd heard in her voice. Who the hell did she think she was, making uninformed judgements about him? She didn't know him. She knew nothing about him or his tastes in women. Yet she was implying he was some moron who could only think with his sex.

The fact that that *was* what he had been doing was not something Liam chose to consider at that moment. 'Be careful, Miss Chantry,' he said unpleasantly. 'I'll begin to think you were disappointed that I stopped when I did.'

'How dare you?'

Rosa didn't think she had ever felt so furious. Her hand

balled into a fist almost automatically, connecting with the hard muscles of his stomach before she had time to reconsider. She suspected she'd hurt herself more than she hurt him, but it didn't matter. He had no right to ridicule her. Not when, for a heart-stopping moment, he'd made her feel so good.

Liam was surprised at the fierceness of her attack. 'You need to control that temper of yours, Miss Chantry,' he panted, annoyed at his shortness of breath. 'What the hell's the matter with you? What did I say to warrant that response?'

'You know what you said, Mr Jameson.' Rosa was trembling, but she refused to back down.

'Yeah?' Some evil demon was urging him on. 'And wasn't it true?'

Rosa stared at him, wondering how she could ever have been attracted to this man. 'You have a much inflated opinion of yourself, Mr Jameson,' she said icily, keeping her voice down with an effort. It would have been so much more satisfying to shout at him. 'If I allowed myself, just for a moment, to give in to you, it was simply because I felt sorry for you. I mean, it can't be much fun living here on your own, with only your female staff for diversion.'

The outrage Liam felt at being unknowingly but callously reminded of Kayla's defection brought a crippling wave of anger sweeping over him. Forgetting that he'd been in the wrong here, that her insults were just a counter-attack to his sarcasm, he grasped her wrists and twisted them behind her back. 'You're just a mine of bitterness, aren't you, Miss Chantry?' he chided scathingly. 'It's no wonder you've never been married. No decent man would put up with a spiteful bitch like you.'

Rosa gulped, the instinct to correct his bald assumption overwhelmed by the alarm she felt at finding herself

locked in his savage embrace. She tried to break free, but
with his hot breath almost stifling her, and his thigh
wedged aggressively between her legs, she was helpless.
They were both breathing rapidly, and for several seconds
a silent battle ensued.

But it wasn't really a battle, Rosa acknowledged weakly.
She was at his mercy and he knew it. Though, strangely,
he didn't appear to appreciate his good fortune. On the
contrary, when his eyes encountered hers, she saw they
were filled with a mixture of confusion and regret.

'Hell,' he said harshly. 'This was not meant to happen.'

'So let me go,' said Rosa a little breathlessly, not entirely
immune to the appeal of those green eyes no matter what
he'd said.

This close, she could also see that silvery scar she'd
noticed earlier. She quivered in spite of herself. How had
he really got that?

'Yeah, I should,' he agreed, distracting her, his gaze
dwelling on her mouth with an intensity that felt practically
physical. 'But you know what?' He shifted against her and
she was almost sure she could feel him hardening. 'I don't
want to. Now, isn't that the damnedest thing?'

A knot twisted in Liam's stomach as he watched her
reaction to his admission. Had she any idea that a wave of
heat and need was drumming through him, making what
had begun as a desire to punish her into an insane urge to
show her what she was missing? He could feel her trembling, even though she was doing her best to hold herself
away from him, and the breasts he'd admired earlier were
now surprisingly urgent against her woollen sweater.

'Please,' Rosa said unsteadily, probably hoping to
appeal to his better judgement. But Liam only heard what

she said as if from a distance. He'd captured both her wrists in one grip now, and brought his free hand round to rub his knuckles against one of those button-hard nipples. He felt her shuddering recoil with a pleasurable rush of blood to his groin.

God, she was responsive, he thought incredulously, wondering how long it had been since she'd had a man. If she'd ever had one, he appended, though he didn't quite believe she was a virgin.

Nevertheless, he wished he'd met her in other circumstances—wished he hadn't antagonised her by being cruel about her unmarried state. Because he was attracted to her, no matter how he might deny it. She wasn't beautiful, of course, but she had a fey charm that appealed to the romantic in him. And there was no denying that he could imagine, only too easily, all that glorious hair spread over the pillow on his bed.

Rosa's legs were beginning to feel as if they wouldn't support her weight for much longer. Liam had turned his attention to her other breast now, covering it with his hand so that the hard peak butted against his palm. The sensation it caused made her feel dizzy, though not as dizzy as getting naked with him would feel, she thought crazily.

Wetness pooled between her legs and she was disconcerted. What was wrong with her? She'd always known, even when Colin was making passionate love to her, that some part of her had stood apart and watched what was going on with a certain objectivity.

But she couldn't be objective with Liam. When he looked at her as he was looking at her now, she couldn't even think straight, let alone anything else. She felt weak, possessed, consumed by needs she'd hardly known existed, so that when he bent his head towards her, her lips parted instinctively for his kiss.

However, although his mouth skimmed the curve of her neck, and the roughness of his jaw grazed her cheek, he didn't kiss her. Well, not on the mouth, anyway. With a feeling of dismay she felt his sudden withdrawal. He let go of her wrists and she stumbled, hardly aware she'd been relying on his support until it was taken away from her.

Then, as she struggled to regain her balance, he turned his back on her and leant on his desk.

CHAPTER SIX

LIAM, MEANWHILE, was hoping she hadn't realised why he'd had to turn away from her. Letting her go hadn't been easy, and his body still wouldn't accept what his mind was telling it to do. Instincts as old at time were demanding satisfaction, but, although the temptation was great, common sense insisted that he had to take control.

Dammit, he reminded himself, apart from the fact that he hardly knew the woman, did he really want to expose himself to ridicule again? Yet when she'd been in his arms, when he'd been breathing her scent, feeling her slim body moving against his, it had been all too easy to delude himself that this might work. All the pheromones in his body had responded to her and he'd so much wanted to bury himself inside her. To find out if she was as tight there as he imagined she would be.

Which, he acknowledged grimly, was crazy. Did he want her to go away from here and tell all her friends what a monster he was? A monster who couldn't keep his pants zipped, he thought bitterly. Yeah, the tabloids would have a field-day with that one.

Of course eventually he had to look behind him. Without the slightly unsteady sound of her breathing he wouldn't

have known she was still there. But she was, and she
deserved some explanation. Though what he was going to
say he wasn't sure.

After checking himself to make sure there was no em-
barrassing bulge in his pants, he turned to face her again.
Her face was still flushed, he noticed, giving her an unexpected beauty, but she was doing her best to behave as if
he hadn't just made a complete prat of himself. God, he
thought, he didn't need this. He had a book to write, for
pity's sake.

Rosa steeled herself as he turned. If he intended to
blame her for what had happened, she had her answer
ready. She hadn't asked him to touch her, and he'd had no
right to treat her with so little respect. Heavens, he still
thought she'd never been married. Goodness knew what he
might have done if he'd known the truth.

If only there was some way to get away from here. If
she had a car, for instance—or the use of a phone—she
wouldn't have had to stand there like a fool, waiting for him
to remember he had a guest. As it was, she was dependent
on him for a phone, both to ring for transport and to call
her mother. She disliked being beholden to him for
anything after what had happened.

Liam sighed. This was a new experience for him, and
he didn't like it. He didn't like it one bit. When he needed
a woman, he found one who knew what she was doing.
He'd never brought any woman here before, never done
anything to violate the atmosphere of his home.

Until now.

Swallowing his pride, he said stiffly, 'I know you're not
going to believe me, but I don't do this sort of thing—'

He would have continued, but Rosa broke in before he

could say anything else. 'You're right,' she said tersely. 'I don't believe you, Mr Jameson. I may be naïve, but you can't tell me you've never taken advantage of a woman before.'

'Dammit!' Liam caught his breath. 'I didn't take advantage of you,' he exclaimed impatiently. 'If I had, you'd know it, and you don't.' He paused. 'And call me Liam, for God's sake. You don't know how ridiculous you sound, calling me Mr Jameson after what just happened. You may still be a virgin, but I'm not.'

That was unforgivable, but he'd had it with trying to humour her. And it wasn't as if she hadn't played some part in the affair. Some part in his downfall, he amended grimly. He wasn't going to forget this in a long time.

'Oh, I'm sure everything about me seems ridiculous to you,' Rosa retorted, stung by his unfair criticism. 'But for your information I *have* been married, Mr Jameson. I divorced my ex-husband over three years ago.'

Liam stared blankly at her. 'You've been married?' he echoed disbelievingly.

'For five years,' she agreed, glad she'd been able to shock him at last.

'You don't look old enough.'

'Well, I am. I'm thirty-two, Mr Jameson. Quite old enough, I assure you.'

Liam was surprised. And disgruntled. He'd put her down as being no more than twenty-five. But he was most disturbed by the way this news affected him. If he'd known how old she really was, and that she'd been married...

But he mustn't go there. Wasn't it enough that he'd made a bloody fool of himself and created an awkward situation for himself into the bargain?

'Look,' he said, tight-lipped, 'let's agree that we've both made some mistakes here. I shouldn't have grabbed you, I admit it. But you shouldn't have made me so mad that I forgot what I was doing.'

Rosa wanted to argue that she hadn't been the one who'd brought her here, that if he'd been honest right from the beginning none of this would have happened. But a reluctant awareness that she hadn't exactly put up much of a fight kept her silent, and when she finally spoke it was to say, 'Would it be all right if I used your phone, then?'

Liam knew a most inappropriate desire to laugh. Her words were so unexpected, so prosaic, as if all they'd been doing for the past half-hour was discussing the weather. But he had the sense to realise that humour would definitely not go down very well at this moment, and with a careless lift of his shoulders he said, 'Why not?'

'Thanks.' Rosa hoped she sounded sincere. 'I just want to ring my mother again.'

Liam arched dark brows. 'And tell her your sister's not here?'

'Yes.'

'Okay.' He nodded towards the desk where the phone was situated. 'Be my guest.'

Rosa hesitated for a moment, feeling awkward now. 'Um—perhaps I could ring for a taxi at the same time?' she ventured. 'What was it you called that man?'

'McAllister?'

Rosa nodded.

'No need.' Liam started for the door, trying to hide the fact that his leg was protesting at the sudden activity. 'Sam's driving over to the village later this morning. You can go with him.'

Rosa wasn't sure she wanted that. Sam Devlin hadn't exactly welcomed her here. 'If it's just the same to you, I'll call McAllister,' she murmured, wishing she didn't have to ask. 'I don't want to put anyone out.'

Liam paused now, half turning to face her, his brows drawing together above those piercing green eyes. 'What's Sam been saying to you?'

'Oh—nothing.' And it was true. 'I'd just—prefer to make my own arrangements.'

Liam regarded her broodingly. 'So you don't want any advice on where to stay?'

'Well—yes.' Rosa hadn't thought of that. 'That would be useful.'

'Okay.' Liam reached for the door. 'I'll have Sam give you an address.' He pulled the door open, trying not to drag his foot as he moved into the aperture. 'Take your time. There's no hurry.'

'Oh, but—'

'Yes?'

His response was clipped, and Rosa, who had been about to ask if he'd injured his leg, changed her mind. 'You—haven't given me Mr McAllister's number,' she said, with sudden inspiration, and Liam frowned.

'I can't remember it off-hand. I'll have Sam give you that, too. After you've rung your mother.'

And wasn't Sam going to wonder why she'd refused to drive back to the village with him? But, 'Okay,' she said weakly. 'Thanks.'

'No problem.' Liam was eager now to put this unfortunate interlude behind him. 'Have a good trip back.'

'Oh—' Once again, Rosa detained him. 'I mean—I will see you again before I leave?'

It had been an inane question, bearing in mind that he'd just wished her a good trip, but, conversely, now that the time had come, Rosa was curiously loath to leave him.

Liam sighed, leaning heavily on the door for support. 'You're not going to tell me you'll be sorry to go, are you?' he asked flatly. 'Because, quite frankly, *I'd* find that hard to believe.'

Rosa met his mocking gaze defensively. Then, to her dismay, she found herself saying, 'I suppose you'll be glad to see the back of me?'

Liam took an audible gulp of air. How was he supposed to answer that?

'Pretty much,' he admitted at last. Then, seeing her expression, he added, 'You're too much of a distraction.'

'Oh, right.' She gave him a scornful look. 'What you mean is, I've wasted too much of your time already.'

Liam shrugged. 'I didn't say that.'

'You didn't have to.' Rosa turned towards the desk. Then, picking up the receiver, she said, 'I hope your leg's better soon.'

Liam blinked, but she wasn't looking at him now. And, although he was tempted to ask her what she knew about his injuries, he kept his mouth shut.

The door closed behind him and Rosa breathed a sigh of relief. The sooner she left here, the better. Despite what she'd thought before, he was dangerous to her peace of mind.

Her mother answered on the second ring, and when she did Rosa was instantly aware of the anticipation in her voice.

'Sophie?' Mrs Chantry said eagerly. 'Oh, darling, I hoped you'd ring back.'

Back?

Rosa was stunned. 'You mean you've heard from her?'

There was a moment's silence. 'Rosa? Rosa, is that you?'

'Who else?' Rosa could hear the edge in her voice but she couldn't help it. 'What's going on, Mum? I gather you've heard from Sophie?'

'Well, yes.' Her mother sighed. 'She rang yesterday evening.' She made a sound of excitement. 'You can't imagine how relieved I was.'

Rosa could. Sophie could do anything and their mother would forgive her. Even if, as in this case, she'd been telling a pack of lies.

'So where is she?' Rosa asked, forcing herself to be patient. 'Did she tell you that?'

'Of course.' Mrs Chantry sounded indignant now. 'She's in Scotland, as she said.' She paused, and then went on breathlessly, 'She's having a wonderful time. Everyone's been so kind to her, and there's every chance she'll get a part in the production. Isn't that amazing?'

'Unbelievable, certainly,' said Rosa drily, wondering if her mother was pathologically foolish where Sophie was concerned. For heaven's sake, who was going to employ a starstruck teenager with a very minimal acting talent?

'I might have known you'd say something like that, Rosa.' Mrs Chantry sounded irritable now. 'Just because Sophie isn't on the island, as you expected, you're taking your frustration out on me. Well, Scotland's a big country. It's natural that a production like this would need a less confined location.'

'It wasn't *my* idea to come to the island,' Rosa pointed out, aware that she sounded peeved. 'It was your idea, not mine.' She paused. 'Did you tell her where I was?'

'Not exactly.'

'You mean you didn't.' Rosa gritted her teeth. 'So where is she?'

'I've just told you. She's in Scotland,' said her mother testily.

'Where in Scotland?'

'Ah…' There was a pregnant pause. 'Well, I'm not precisely sure.'

'But you said you'd heard from her.'

'I have. I did.' Mrs Chantry sighed. 'But you know what Sophie's like, Rosa. She was so busy telling me all the exciting things that have happened to her that she forgot about giving me her address.'

'I'll bet.'

'Oh, don't be like that, Rosa. Can't you find out where she is?'

Rosa sighed. 'How am I supposed to do that?'

'Well, you said Liam Jameson was there, didn't you? He'll know.'

'Mum…' It was growing increasingly hard to be patient. 'There *is* no film production. Or, if there is, Liam Jameson doesn't know about it.'

'Have you asked him?'

'I—er—'

Belatedly, Rosa acknowledged that that was something that they hadn't discussed. When she'd found out Sophie wasn't on the island, that there was no film crew working there, she hadn't thought to ask if he'd given permission for a film to be made elsewhere.

But wouldn't he have told her?

Yet he hadn't told her who he was until he'd had to.

She'd been silent for too long, and her mother said sharply, 'You *have* spoken to him, haven't you?'

Spoken?

Rosa stifled the hysterical sob that rose in her throat at her mother's words. Yes, she'd spoken to him all right, she thought. Though that was a poor description of what had happened between them.

'Yes,' she said, her voice a little hoarse. 'I've spoken to him, Mum. He was very—nice, actually.' And that had to be the understatement of the year!

'And he insisted he'd never seen Sophie?' Mrs Chantry sounded anxious now, and Ross wished she hadn't been so brutal. 'Oh, I wish she'd taken her phone with her to Glastonbury. But Mark was taking his, and I was so afraid she'd lose it.'

'I—I don't think Jameson's seen her,' Rosa murmured weakly, hating the thought that her mother was going to start worrying all over again. 'I—I'll ask him again.'

'Oh, you're a good girl, Rosa.' Now that she thought her daughter was softening, Mrs Chantry was prepared to be generous. 'I knew I could rely on you. And don't forget to find out where the film is being made.'

Rosa put the phone down with a feeling of utter bewilderment. Speaking to her mother was like butting her head against a brick wall. Mrs Chantry only heard what she wanted to hear, and now that Rosa had agreed to speak to Liam Jameson again she was prepared to wait for developments.

Rosa swore—something she rarely did, but right now she felt it was justified. Wait until she got her hands on her younger sister, she thought. Sophie would regret putting them through all this trauma.

Yet if Sophie hadn't disappeared Rosa wouldn't have come here, wouldn't have met Liam Jameson for herself. And, while that was something she might live to regret, right now the prospect of seeing him again was causing her heart to beat so madly it felt as if it was in danger of forcing its way right out of her chest.

But where had he gone?

She crossed to the door and pulled it open, only to fall back in surprise when she found Sam Devlin just outside. Had he been listening in to her conversation?

But, no. Something told her that the burly Scotsman wouldn't be interested in anything she had to say, and this was confirmed when he said brusquely, 'Yon McAllister's on his way from the village. He should be here in about half an hour. Would you like me to carry your bag down for you?'

'Oh—no.' Rosa was taken aback. But she should have known that Sam would waste no time in sending her on her way. 'That won't be necessary.' She paused. 'Actually, I wanted to have a word with Mr Jameson before I go.'

'I'm afraid that's impossible, Miss Chantry. Mr Jameson is working, and it's more than my job's worth to disturb him.'

Rosa doubted that very much. From what she'd seen, the two men had a good working relationship, and it was extremely unlikely that Liam Jameson would risk that by threatening to sack Devlin if he was disturbed.

'It would only take a minute,' she said persuasively. 'I want to ask him something.'

'I'm sorry.'

Sam wasn't budging, and Rosa stared at him in frustration. If only she knew where Liam's office—*den*?—was. Evidently he didn't work in the library, as she'd thought at first. But in a place of this size he could be anywhere.

'Tell me what you want to ask him and I'll deliver your

message when he's free,' Sam suggested, but Rosa had no intention of trusting him.

'It's personal,' she said, but although she held the man's gaze for a long while, hoping to shame him into helping her, ultimately it was she who looked away.

Then another thought occurred to her. 'You could give me his phone number,' she said with inspiration. 'I'll ring him later.'

'I couldn't do that, Miss Chantry.'

'Why not?'

'Mr Jameson doesn't give his private number to anyone.'

'Then give me yours,' mumbled Rosa ungraciously. 'I'll let you know where I'm staying, and Mr Jameson can ring me.'

Sam looked as if he wanted to refuse, but perhaps he realised that that would seem unnecessarily anal. Besides, he couldn't really know that Liam wouldn't speak to her if he went and asked him.

However, when he spoke it wasn't what Rosa had expected. 'Mr Jameson knows where you're staying, Miss Chantry,' he said, and now Rosa noticed the scrap of paper in his hand. 'He asked me to give you this address.'

'Oh!' That stumped her. 'Thanks.' She took the paper from his outstretched hand and looked at it almost resentfully. 'Does Mr McAllister know where this is?'

'Everyone knows where Katie Ferguson's guesthouse is,' declared Sam scornfully. 'This isn't London, Miss Chantry.'

'I don't live in London,' retorted Rosa hotly. 'I come from a small town in North Yorkshire, Mr Devlin. Not some teeming metropolis, as you seem to think.'

'I'm sorry.' Rosa was sure he didn't mean it. 'I naturally assumed—'

'You shouldn't assume anything,' said Rosa, enjoying having him on the defensive for a change. She glanced down at the paper again. 'Thanks for this.'

Sam gave her a polite nod of acknowledgement. 'I'll let you know when the car arrives.'

'Thanks,' said Rosa again, and without another word Sam closed the door on her.

CHAPTER SEVEN

'HAS SHE GONE?'

It was later that morning, and Liam had just emerged from his study having spent a rather fruitless couple of hours trying to concentrate on characters who suddenly seemed as unconvincing as cardboard cut-outs.

He'd found Sam and Mrs Wilson in the kitchen on the ground floor of the castle, enjoying a coffee break, and he'd accepted a cup from the housekeeper with some gratitude.

He wasn't in the best of moods, however, and his temper wasn't improved when Sam said cheerfully, 'Aye, she's gone, Liam. Not but what she didn't ask to speak to you again before she left.' He gave his employer a knowing look. 'I told her you were working and couldn't be disturbed, but I don't think she was suited.'

Liam scowled. He'd just burned his mouth on the hot coffee, and Sam's announcement was the last straw. 'You did what?' he demanded harshly. 'Why did you tell her that?'

'Well, because you never like to be disturbed when you're working,' said Sam defensively. 'Don't tell me you expected me to come along to your office and break your concentration just because some lassie with more bluff than sense asked to see you?'

'I beg your pardon?'

Liam's scowl deepened, and Mrs Wilson made a hasty exit through the back door, murmuring something about needing some greens from the garden. Meanwhile, Sam stared at the younger man belligerently, although his face reddened with colour. 'I think you heard what I said,' he muttered defiantly.

'And who appointed you my guardian?' exclaimed Liam, equally unprepared to back down. 'I know you didn't like me bringing her here. You made that plain enough. But this is my house, Devlin, not yours.'

Sam straightened. He had been lounging against the drainer as he chatted with the housekeeper, but now he stiffened his back. 'I thought I was doing you a favour, man,' he protested. He lifted an apologetic hand. 'Obviously I was wrong. I'm sorry. Rest assured, it won't happen again.'

He turned and thrust his cup into the sink, but when he started across the room, evidently intending to leave Liam to it, Liam stepped into his path.

'No, *I'm* sorry,' he said roughly, ashamed at taking his frustration out on the older man. 'Forget what I said, Sam. It's not your fault I'm in a bloody mood.'

Sam hesitated, still looking upset, and Liam cursed himself anew for distressing him. Dammit, Sam was right. He probably *would* have complained if Sam had interrupted him. He was letting a woman he might never see again ruin the long-established relationship he had with his steward, and that was stupid.

'I mean it,' he grunted, holding out his hand. 'Take no notice of me. I've had a pretty useless morning, and I'm ready to blame anyone but myself.'

Sam's jaw clenched, but he took Liam's hand and shook

it warmly. 'Yon lassie's to blame,' he said staunchly, but Liam wasn't prepared to go that far.

'Well, she's gone now,' he said neutrally, taking another mouthful of his coffee and finding it more to his taste. 'McAllister turned up, I gather?'

'Aye. In that old rattletrap he calls an estate car,' agreed Sam, relaxing now. 'How it passes its MOT test, God knows!'

'I don't suppose it does,' said Liam, hoping it hadn't broken down between Kilfoil and the village. He was remembering what Rosa had said about the dangers of the moor, and to imagine her walking into one of its treacherous bogs was enough to bring another scowl to his lips.

But he wasn't about to bring that up with Sam, and, finishing his coffee, he said, 'I'll see you later. I'm going to take the dogs out.'

Sam arched his grey brows. 'Shall I come with you?' He eyed his employer's injured thigh with concerned eyes. 'You don't want to have another of those spasms when you're out on the cliffs.'

Liam hid his impatience at the other man's fussing, and said evenly, 'The physio says I should get plenty of exercise. He says that spending too long at my desk is probably the reason why I'm still having problems.'

'Even so—'

'I'll be fine,' Liam assured him tersely. 'But thanks for the offer.'

After collecting a coat, and the dogs, Liam emerged into the open air with a feeling of relief. The animals were just as glad to escape the confines of the castle, and they ran about excitedly, chasing every cat and bird in sight.

Liam didn't intend to go far. There were clouds massing on the horizon, and unless he missed his guess they'd have rain before nightfall. Knowing how quickly the weather could change in these parts, he had no desire to risk getting caught in a storm. He could be soaked to the skin in minutes. It wasn't as if he could run for cover, either. Thanks to his attacker, his running days were over.

Even so, he went out onto the cliffs, trudging through knee-high grasses that were an ideal hiding place for small rodents and birds of all kinds. The wind, blowing off the ocean, lifted the thick dark hair from his forehead and made him wish he'd worn something warmer than the ankle-length waterproof coat that flapped around his legs.

His thigh did move more freely as he exercised it, but he didn't think he was up to negotiating the cliff steps down to the cove this morning. Climbing down necessitated climbing up again, and that was probably a step too far.

He was considering turning back when Harley, the younger of the two retrievers, scared up a rabbit. The terrified creature must have been hiding in the gorse bushes that grew near the edge of the cliff, and when Harley started barking it shot away across the headland, making unmistakably for the gully that ran down to the beach.

Naturally, Harley gave chase, pursued by the other dogs, and although Liam shouted himself hoarse he soon realised he was wasting his time. The dogs weren't going to come back until the rabbit had been rousted, and it was at that moment that he felt the first heavy drops of rain.

He swore loudly, limping across to the edge of the cliffs. He could see all three dogs from this vantage point. The gully was a lot easier for a dog to negotiate than the steps, and, although there was no sign of the rabbit, the dogs were having a whale of a time racing along the sand, splashing in and out of the waves breaking on the shore.

'Dammit!' He swore again, but although he tried every way he could to get them to come back they weren't listening to him.

What price now his arrogant assertion that he didn't need Sam's help? he thought grimly. The man might be fifteen years older than Liam, but he wouldn't have thought twice about going after the dogs. And, unless he wanted to return home with his own metaphoric tail between his legs, Liam knew he'd have to do the same.

It wasn't too bad going down. Although the rain was getting heavier, his determination kept him going—until his boots sank into the damp sand. The dogs came to him eagerly now, barking and leaping around him, as if their aim had been to get him down there all along.

'Home,' ordered Liam grimly, ignoring their welcome, and at last his tone had some success. Or maybe it was the rain, he reflected wryly. It was certainly quite a downpour, and even the dogs preferred a dry coat to a wet one. Whatever the reason, all three of them obeyed his command, charging up the steps ahead of him, standing at the top, panting and wagging their tails with apparent pride at their achievement.

However, Liam found it much harder to follow them. The steps were slippery now, and every now and then, he was forced to clutch at handfuls of turf to prevent himself from sliding backwards.

His thigh ached, and halfway up he had to stop and allow the spasms in his leg to subside. God, he should have swallowed his pride and gone back to the castle for help, he thought bitterly. The way his muscles were feeling now, he'd probably undone all the good that treatment he'd had in London had achieved.

The dogs had disappeared by the time he finally reached the clifftop. Which was par for the course, he thought, panting heavily. He just hoped they'd gone back to the castle. If they hadn't, hard luck. He wasn't going looking for them. He was just relieved that Rosa Chantry wasn't still there. He'd have hated for her to see him like this. Dammit, he still had some pride.

It rained all day Wednesday.

Rosa, who was confined to Katie Ferguson's guesthouse, stared out at the weather with a feeling of desperation. She felt so helpless. Where was Sophie? she fretted, the inactivity putting her at the mercy of her fears. All right, she'd said she was okay, and Rosa had to accept that. But something about this whole situation didn't add up.

Still, she could do nothing until the ferry arrived the following morning, she consoled herself, rubbing a circle in the condensation her breath had made on the glass. The guesthouse was cosy, her room small, but comfortable. But there were no other guests with whom she could have passed the time.

She glanced across the room at the table beside the bed. Two paperbacks that she'd bought at the post office-cum-general store resided there. One was a historical romance with a Scottish setting that she'd hoped might distract her from her troubles, but it hadn't. The other was a Liam Jameson.

The postmistress, a rather garrulous Scotswoman, had gone on at some length about the quality of Liam's writing. She'd read everything he'd ever written, she'd said, even though she didn't usually enjoy that sort of thing.

'But his characters are so good, aren't they?' she'd

enthused. 'That Luther Killian! My goodness, I'd never realised that vampires could be so fascinating.'

Of course Rosa had had to admit that she hadn't read any of Liam's books, and that was when she'd discovered how Sam had explained her presence on the island.

'Why, I was sure you'd have read all of them, seeing as you work for his publisher and all,' the postmistress had exclaimed in surprise. And when Rosa had looked confused she'd added ruefully, 'Och, old McAllister told us who you were. When Sam Devlin called him out to Kilfoil, he said a young lady from Pargeters had been visiting Mr Jameson.' She'd nodded at the rain. 'It's only a pity you're seeing the island in its worst light. It's really quite beautiful.'

Rosa had admitted then that it hadn't been raining when she'd first arrived. But, not wanting to contribute to any more gossip, she'd paid for the books and made good her escape.

However, she wondered now if Sam had told Mrs Ferguson the same story. It seemed possible, although her landlady was much more reserved, and she hadn't questioned why Rosa should have been visiting the castle.

Rosa sighed. Nevertheless, it was because of Liam that she'd found it impossible to read his book. She couldn't help associating Luther Killian with the man who'd created him, and the fact that Liam hadn't bothered getting back to her was a constant thorn in her side.

Not that she'd told her mother that. She'd rung Mrs Chantry on Tuesday evening to let her know where she was staying, giving her the phone number of the guesthouse as if she'd never stayed anywhere else. She'd promised she'd be speaking to Jameson again the following day, leaving her mother with the impression that another interview had been arranged.

Fortunately Mrs Chantry hadn't questioned that, and Rosa hadn't talked for long. Apart from anything else, she'd been conscious that Mrs Ferguson could come into the small hallway where the phone was situated at any time, and the last thing Rosa wanted was for her to suspect that her reasons for being here weren't what she'd heard.

All in all, it had been a miserable couple of days. The rain had started soon after she and Mr McAllister had left the castle the previous morning, and his old estate car had taken for ever to cross the moor. Then, coming down into the village, they'd skidded onto the grass verge, so that Rosa had been relieved when she'd arrived safely at her destination.

Leaving her seat by the window, Rosa crossed the room and picked up Liam's book. There was still an hour to fill before supper, which appeared to be served early in the Highlands. And another couple of hours after that before she could reasonably retire to bed. She had to do something.

Of course what she ought to do was hire old McAllister's cab again and drive back to the castle, if only to keep the promise she'd made to her mother. Liam wasn't going to ring her, either because Sam hadn't given him her message or because he chose not to, and this might be her last chance.

But the idea of chancing another ride in the elderly estate car filled her with unease. And, apart from that, she didn't really have a reason for seeing Liam again. Not a genuine one, at any rate. Wanting to spend a little more time with him just didn't cut it, particularly after he'd admitted that he'd be glad to see her go. So she might as well resign herself to another night at the guesthouse and a trip back to the mainland tomorrow afternoon.

But the following morning Rosa awakened to the sound of the wind howling round the walls of the old building. Snuggling under the covers, she wished she didn't have to get out of bed. It sounded more like a gale than anything, and she could just imagine being on the ferry in such a wind. Goodness, she'd felt sick coming here, and the water had been reasonably calm then. Now it was going to be as choppy as a bathtub. Or rather the ferry would be as helpless as a bathtub in a turbulent sea.

Rosa sighed, but there was no help for it. She had to get up. Mrs Ferguson had told her that the ferry usually arrived at about half-past-eleven and then left again at half-past-twelve, calling at the nearby island of Ardnarossa before returning to Mallaig.

Which meant at least another hour on her journey, thought Rosa dismally. Another hour in weather like this! She was going to be so seasick. She wished she dared feign illness and stay until the following Monday, when the ferry came again.

But it wasn't in her nature to lie, and she owed it to her mother to get back to the mainland and try and find out from the Scottish Tourist Office if they knew anything about the company Sophie professed to have joined. It was a doubtful proposition, but it was the only one she had at the moment. And right now the idea of being back on the mainland again sounded pretty good to her.

However, after washing and dressing and packing her bag, she went downstairs for breakfast to find Mrs Ferguson waiting for her.

'I'm afraid you won't be leaving today, Miss Chantry,'

she said apologetically. 'This storm has suspended all sailings, and the ferry won't be leaving Mallaig until it's blown itself out.'

The relief Rosa felt was paralysing. 'You mean, I'll have to stay here until the wind's dropped?'

'Well, until it moderates, at least,' Mrs Ferguson agreed with a regretful smile. 'I'm sorry.'

'It's not your fault.' Rosa was ashamed to realise she could hardly contain her relief. 'So—um, when do you think the storm will blow itself out?'

'Not before Saturday, at the earliest,' said the landlady sagely. 'And even then there's no guarantee that the ferry will come. We're just a small island, Miss Chantry. They may decide to wait until the regular sailing on Monday.'

'Monday!' Rosa thought ruefully that you really should be careful what you wish for. 'I see.'

'Of course, if there's an urgent reason why you need to get back to the mainland, you could always ask Mr Jameson. He might be willing to have his pilot take you in his helicopter. I mean…' Mrs Ferguson seemed to be considering the situation '…he *is* the reason why you're stuck here, isn't he?'

'Y-e-s.' Rosa drew the word out, knowing that her reasons for being here and the reasons Mrs Ferguson had probably been given for her being here were mutually exclusive. 'But I don't think that's a good idea.' As the landlady looked as if she was about to protest, she added swiftly, 'Don't helicopters have problems in bad weather, too?'

'Not like ferries,' Mrs Ferguson assured her. 'I'm sure that by tomorrow you'd have no trouble at all.'

Wouldn't she? Rosa doubted that. There was no way Liam would lend his helicopter—a helicopter, for heaven's sake!—to her. It was just another indication of how stupid she was being in wanting to see him again. His way of life was so incredibly different from hers.

However, she refrained from making any comment, and the landlady bustled away to get her guest's breakfast. Mrs Ferguson was probably thinking she was considering it, thought Rosa, with a grimace. When in fact what she was really thinking was that this might give her another opportunity to speak to Liam again.

CHAPTER EIGHT

FAT CHANCE, thought Rosa on Friday morning, having spent yet another day watching the rain. She had borrowed a coat from Mrs Ferguson and gone out for a while on Thursday afternoon, but it hadn't been much fun. The rain had been bad enough, but the wind had been unforgiving. It had torn back the hood of her coat and had left her hair at the mercy of the weather.

She'd even made another attempt to read Liam's book, and had been enjoying it until Luther Killian said something that Liam himself might say. It had brought back the memory of their encounter in all its disturbing detail, and she'd had to put the book aside and do something else.

Looking out of her window now, Rosa saw that it was going to be another wasted day. The wind hardly seemed to have eased at all, and although the rain seemed lighter, it was still coming down.

She could see the harbour from her window, the small boats that were moored there straining on their lines. No doubt the fishermen whose boats they were, were cursing, too. At least her incarceration didn't affect her livelihood.

Or Sophie's, she thought uneasily. But her sister would be all right, she assured herself. She was probably sitting

in some luxury hotel at this moment, having a late breakfast with this man she'd taken off with. Okay, he wasn't
Liam Jameson. But perhaps he'd told her that he was. Yet
somehow she knew Sophie was too savvy to be taken in
like that.

So where was she? Although Rosa was fairly sure Liam
didn't know, perhaps he might have an idea. Anything was
better than sitting here, twiddling her thumbs.

She shook her head impatiently, aware that she was
only looking for excuses to go and see him again. After all,
whatever happened, her mother expected her to do it. Pre-
dictably, it was the first thing she'd asked Rosa when she'd
phoned home the previous evening.

'But why haven't you seen him?' she'd demanded, and
Rosa had explained about the storm. Then she'd hurried
on and asked if Mrs Chantry had heard from Sophie—
which she hadn't—to avoid the comeback. After all, it
was her sister who was supposed to be in trouble here,
not her.

Personally, Rosa thought her sister was keeping quiet
deliberately. Now that she'd alerted them to the fact that
she could phone, she was probably afraid they'd trace her
call. Which left Rosa with the unenviable task of finding
another way to locate her.

Her mother was woefully ignorant of her elder daughter's circumstances, however. 'Surely there must be some
other way to get back to the mainland?' she'd protested,
when Rosa had told her that the ferries were suspended
until further notice. 'What about aeroplanes? They're not
grounded, are they? Or you could find another boat.'

Rosa had been stunned at her foolishness. 'There's no
airport on Kilfoil, Mum,' she'd told her frustratedly.

'And what other boat would you suggest? A fishing trawler, perhaps?'

Mrs Chantry had tutted impatiently. 'So you're telling me there's nothing you can do until the ferries start running again?'

'As far as getting off the island is concerned, yes,' said Rosa shortly. 'Believe me, I don't like it any more than you do.'

But was that strictly true? Rosa asked herself now, aware that the knowledge that Liam was just a dozen miles away was some compensation. If the ferries had been running she'd have been several hundred miles away by now, and any chance of seeing him again would have been denied her.

She frowned. Well, she couldn't stay in her room all day. She'd had her breakfast, and once again the books she'd bought held no appeal. There must be some other way she could get out to the castle, she thought, her pulse quickening at the thought. At least it would give her something to do. Even if that old grouse Sam Devlin refused to let her in.

Mrs Ferguson was dusting the sitting room when she went downstairs and, feeling a little awkward, Rosa stopped in the doorway. 'Um—I was wondering,' she said, and the landlady looked up expectantly. 'I was wondering if there was a car I could hire for the day.'

'Do you not know McAllister's number?' The woman frowned and put her duster aside. 'I think I've got it here somewhere—'

'No.' Rosa interrupted her, and when the landlady halted uncertainly, she added, 'I didn't mean a taxi, Mrs Ferguson. I wondered if there was a car I could hire to drive myself.'

The woman frowned. 'Well, it's not much of a day for sightseeing.'

'I know that.' Rosa sighed. 'As a matter of fact, I'd like to drive over to see Mr Jameson again. There—er—there's something I forgot to ask him.'

'Ah.' Mrs Ferguson nodded. 'And you're not keen to have old McAllister drive you, is that it?'

'Well…'

Rosa felt her face turn red, but the landlady was smiling. 'Yes, I can see you're not impressed with his driving, lassie.' She laughed. 'I have to admit, I'd think twice about getting in his vehicle myself.'

Rosa relaxed. 'So—er—*is* there a car I could hire?' she asked hopefully. 'I'm willing to pay.'

'Och, you can take my car, Miss Chantry. It hardly gets used, anyway. It's not very grand, mind you, but it's roadworthy.'

Rosa gasped. 'Oh, that would be wonderful!'

Mrs Ferguson laughed again. 'Don't say that until you've seen it, lassie,' she advised. 'Come along. I'll show you where I keep it.'

The car, an ancient Ford, was kept in a shed at the back of the guesthouse, and Rosa saw at once that the landlady hadn't been exaggerating when she'd said it wasn't very grand. It had to be at least twenty years old, and was covered in dust into the bargain. Mrs Ferguson had to wipe away a handful of spiders' webs before she could open the door.

But the engine started after only a couple of hiccoughs, and Rosa stepped aside as the woman reversed it out onto the street. One good thing—the rain quickly cleared the dust from the chassis, and Rosa saw that the wipers worked. All in all, it was exactly what she needed, and she couldn't thank the landlady enough.

'Och, it's nothing,' said Mrs Ferguson, surrendering the

driving seat to her guest and stepping back into the shelter of the shed, out of the rain. 'You drive carefully, now. The roads can be treacherous in the wet. I wouldn't like you to go skidding into a bog.'

Rosa thought she wouldn't like that, either, but she refused to be daunted. She couldn't be a worse driver than old McAllister if she tried. And there was no hurry. If she took all morning to get there, it wouldn't matter.

The first indication that driving Mrs Ferguson's car wasn't going to be a sinecure came when Rosa reached the first corner and tried to turn. The wheel was like a dead weight in her hands, and she realised that it had no power steering. Of course, she thought impatiently, wrenching the car round manually. The installation of power steering in small cars like this was a comparatively recent innovation.

It made driving much harder, and her arms were aching by the time she'd negotiated the twists and turns down to the harbour. It was easier once she was driving up the road out of the village, but she wasn't looking forward to the journey across that lonely stretch of moor.

The rain hindered visibility, too, and once or twice she was sure she saw ghostly figures rising out of the mist. But it was only the skeletal trunks of trees worn bare by the winds that raked the boggy scrubland. Nevertheless, she was glad she didn't have to drive across here in the dark.

At last she reached the road that wound down into the glen where Kilfoil Castle was situated. She couldn't see the castle, of course. The driving rain made that impossible. But now and then she glimpsed a farmhouse, and the unmistakable presence of livestock. She even saw a farmer herding some cows into a barn.

She relaxed. She'd made it. The only problem now was

getting in to see Liam himself. She had the feeling Sam wouldn't be too pleased when she presented herself at the door. But he must know she hadn't left the island. Surely he might expect that she'd try to see his employer again?

She drove over the small bridge and parked in the same place Liam had used four days ago. Four days! She was amazed. Was that really all it was? She grimaced. Sometimes it felt as if she'd been here half her life.

She got out of the car, closing the door with care. No one had come to meet her, and she was curiously loath to announce her arrival in advance. Squaring her shoulders against the squally wind that blew in off the ocean, she crossed the forecourt to the double doors.

There was no bell, but she'd hardly expected one. Knights of old hadn't needed such things. In the books she'd read, the knight's lady would be watching for her spouse from one of the narrow windows in the solar, or perhaps a vigilant guard would warn of a stranger's arrival. The portcullis would be lowered to protect those within the castle—

'Miss Chantry!'

Rosa had been so absorbed with her thoughts that she hadn't heard the door being opened. But now the housekeeper stood there, regarding her with obvious surprise.

'Oh, Mrs Wilson.' Rosa knew she should have been better prepared for this encounter. 'Um—how are you?'

'I'm very well, thank you.' The woman cast a nervous glance over her shoulder. 'Is there something I can help you with, Miss Chantry?'

'I hope so, yes.' Rosa smiled. 'Is—er—is Mr Jameson about?'

It was a stupid question. Rosa knew that as soon as the words left her lips. Where else would he be?

'Mr Jameson?'

The housekeeper sounded doubtful, and she hurried on, 'Yes. I mean, is he working this morning? Or could I have a quick word with him?'

'Oh, I—' Once again Mrs Wilson looked back over her shoulder. 'I'm afraid that's not a question I can answer, Miss Chantry.' She hesitated, and then went on, 'You'd have to ask Mr Devlin.' She nodded. 'I'll get him for you.'

'No, I—'

Rosa started to say Sam Devlin was the last person she wanted to see, but it was too late. The woman had already turned and hurried away, leaving Rosa to cool her heels on the doorstep like some pushy double-glazing saleswoman.

She could have invited her inside, Rosa thought, disheartened. It wasn't as if she hadn't been inside the castle before. For heaven's sake, she'd spent a night here. Why was she being treated like an intruder?

Because that was what she was, she'd decided, when she heard Sam Devlin's footsteps crossing the hall. She'd just nudged under the overhang, in a rather fruitless attempt to keep dry, but she stepped aback almost instinctively when the man appeared.

However, Sam was surprisingly more charitable than the housekeeper. 'Och, come away inside, Miss Chantry,' he exclaimed, stepping back to allow her to enter the huge hall. 'It's a wretched morning, to be sure. You'll be wishing this storm would ease, no doubt. I dare say you're eager to get back to the mainland?'

'Yes.' Rosa had little option other than to agree. 'Um, I'm sorry to trouble you again, but I still haven't spoken to Mr Jameson.' She paused, and then went on rather recklessly, 'You did give him my message, didn't you?'

'What message would that be, Miss Chantry?'

Rosa sighed. She should have known his charity wouldn't stretch that far. 'Well, that I wanted to speak to him again,' she said stiffly. 'If the ferry hadn't been delayed, I'd be gone by now.'

'So you would.' Sam regarded her consideringly as he closed the heavy door. 'But, contrary to what you believe, Miss Chantry, I *did* tell Mr Jameson what you'd said.'

'Oh. Oh, I see.' Rosa felt foolish now, and her face burned with sudden colour. 'What you mean is, Mr Jameson didn't want to speak to me, is that right?' She swallowed her humiliation. 'Well, that's all right. I realise now I shouldn't have bothered him.' She turned back to the door. 'Thank you for telling me.'

'Wait!' As she fumbled with the latch, Sam spoke again. 'Look, Miss Chantry,' he said, and now he sounded a little embarrassed, 'I didn't mean to imply that Liam had refused to speak to you. As a matter of fact I don't know what he might have done if—if…' He hesitated, as if he didn't want to go on, but courtesy demanded it. 'If he'd been able,' he finished at last. Then, after another pause, 'He—er—he hasn't been too well since you left on Tuesday. And that's the truth.'

Rosa was dismayed at the effect his words had on her. 'Is it his leg?' she asked, realising she was stepping onto unknown ground, but anxious enough to take the risk. She linked her cold fingers, pressing them at right angles to her chest. 'Please—tell me.'

Sam frowned. 'You know about his injuries?' he asked warily, but Rosa wasn't brave enough to claim that.

'Just—just that he seems to be troubled at times,' she admitted, shifting from one foot to the other. She stared at him. 'Doesn't he?'

'Perhaps.' Sam was noncommittal. 'But as it happens he got soaked when he was out with the dogs on Tuesday afternoon, and since then he hasn't felt very sociable.'

'You mean he got a chill?'

Sam was evidently unhappy talking about his employer behind his back. 'Something like that,' he admitted at last. 'As you've learned to your cost, the weather here can be unpredictable.'

'You don't mean it developed into pneumonia?' exclaimed Rosa, aghast, and Sam gave a helpless shake of his head.

'Och, no,' he said half impatiently. 'Nothing so dramatic. Just a—nasty cold, is all.' He paused, and then added ruefully, 'Liam's no' a good patient, Miss Chantry.'

'Do you want to tell me what the hell's going on?'

The unexpected sound of Liam's voice caused them both to start in alarm, and Sam instantly looked as guilty as hell. 'God, man,' he protested in a shaken voice. 'Do you have to scare us half to death? I didn't hear you.'

'Obviously not.' Liam left his position at the foot of the tower stairs and walked heavily towards them. He noticed that Rosa was looking as if he was the last person she'd expected to see, and that annoyed the hell out of him. This was his house, dammit. Who had she expected to see? 'What's happening?'

Rosa gazed at him in total confusion. After what Sam had been saying, she'd imagined Liam weak and vulnerable, worn out by coughing and sneezing and blowing his nose.

But the reality was much different. In his usual tight jeans, the fabric worn almost white in places she wasn't supposed to look, and a long-sleeved silk shirt, the colour of which exactly matched his eyes, he looked darkly disturbing—and just as dangerous as Luther Killian, she was sure.

'Miss Chantry——' began Sam, but Rosa knew she couldn't allow the older man to take the blame for her intrusion.

'I came to see you,' she broke in quickly, allowing her arms to fall to her sides. 'Mr Devlin was just telling me that—that you hadn't been well.'

'I just told her you had a cold,' exclaimed Sam swiftly, and Rosa wondered at the look that passed between the two men at that moment. 'That's all.'

'Yeah.' Liam accepted his explanation. Whatever faults he might have, Sam was excessively loyal. He wouldn't talk about Liam's private affairs with anyone.

He returned his gaze to Rosa, noticing that she was shivering now. But whether that was because she was only wearing a light jacket or because he'd frightened her, he couldn't be sure. 'Well, Miss Chantry,' he said pleasantly. 'You'd better come with me.'

Rosa's eyes were wide and anxious. 'All right,' she said, giving Sam a grateful look. 'Thanks for your help, Mr Devlin.'

Sam stiffened. 'It was my pleasure, Miss Chantry,' he insisted. Then, as she started after Liam, 'Will you be wanting a lift later?'

'Oh, no.' Rosa gave him a tight smile. 'I borrowed Mrs Ferguson's car. But thanks, anyway.'

Sam nodded, then, addressing himself to his employer, he added, 'Will I ask Mrs Wilson to bring coffee?'

'Sounds like a plan,' agreed Liam, and Sam gave her another searching look before disappearing through a door below the tapestries at the side of the hall.

'You've made a conquest,' remarked Liam drily, gesturing for her to precede him up the stairs, and she frowned.

'I don't think so.'

'I do. Sam's not usually so talkative, believe me. Not with women, anyway.'

Rosa shook her head, starting up the stairs. Following her, Liam was intensely aware of the rounded curve of her bottom swaying with every step she climbed. She might be slim, but she was shapely, her legs long and graceful beneath the close-fitting woollen pants she was wearing.

He also noticed that she'd attempted to pile her glorious hair into a knot on top of her head this morning. But, as usual, the wind and rain had hampered her efforts. Already strands of dark red silk coiled seductively on the shoulders of her jacket, and he was tempted to pick one up and allow it to curl about his fingers.

But he refused to go there. The end result of such an action was not one he wanted to explore, however appealing his own satisfaction might be. Besides, although he was fairly sure she'd been a willing recipient of his attentions earlier in the week, once she'd seen the ugly scars that marred his body she'd probably run as fast as Kayla had done.

Rosa, meanwhile, hearing the sudden hoarseness of his breathing, decided that Sam hadn't been exaggerating when he'd told her Liam had had a cold. He sounded as if he was struggling for breath, and she felt ashamed for doubting him.

They reached the top of the stairs at last, and Liam went ahead along the narrow landing. They passed several doors, including the library and the dining hall that Rosa remembered from her previous visit, and stopped before a door at the end of the hall.

It opened into a large living room. Because of the lowering skies, lamps had been lit on tables and cabinets, several tall uplighters adding illumination to a room that was both beautiful and homely.

A pair of plush suede sofas flanked the carved façade of the fireplace, and bookshelves filled with novels and magazines filled the space beneath the long windows. Raw silk curtains, in the same warm caramel colour as the sofas, were drawn back to display the fury of the storm outside, but Rosa guessed that in fine weather the view would be breathtaking.

Underfoot, a huge Turkish rug in shades of blue and green complemented the heavy-textured wall coverings, which reminded her they were in a castle, not a millionaire's mansion. Though the distinction escaped her.

'Go ahead,' said Liam, stepping back to allow her to enter, and Rosa hesitated.

'My shoes are damp,' she murmured, glancing down, and Liam arched sardonic brows.

'I can see that,' he said with a shrug. 'So take them off.'

'You don't mind?'

'Why would I mind?' Liam queried mockingly. 'Take off anything you like.' He paused, aware that she was looking at him warily now, before adding smoothly, 'Your jacket? It's wet, too.'

CHAPTER NINE

ROSA didn't quite know how to take his flippancy, but she bent and removed her low-heeled shoes, placing them just outside the door. Her jacket she took off, but folded it over her arm. Then, with a strangely fatalistic feeling, she stepped into the room.

The carpet was soft and warm after her damp shoes. She hadn't realised how cold her feet were until she felt the warmth of the room enveloping her from head to toe. She was aware of Liam following her, and when the door closed behind him she swung round with an almost guilty feeling of relief.

'This is a beautiful room,' she said, needing to say something, if only to show he didn't intimidate her. 'The whole castle is beautiful. You're very lucky to live here.'

'Am I?' Liam lifted her coat from her arm and gestured towards the sofas. 'Well, why don't we sit down and talk about it?'

Rosa didn't have an answer for that, but, after watching him drop her jacket onto a chair by the door, she decided she had nothing to lose. Moving round the end of one of the creamy sofas, she perched rather nervously on the edge of the seat.

Liam came to join her, and once again she couldn't help noticing how he dragged his left leg. But she wasn't here to ask personal questions, she reminded herself, though her desire to keep her cool took a bit of a tumble when he chose to sit beside her.

'Okay,' he said, and she was forced to turn in her seat to face him, which caused her to slip a little further back on the cushions. 'So,' he said, 'you've changed your mind?'

'Changed my mind?' Rosa was nonplussed.

'About this place only being good enough for sheep and cattle,' remarked Liam mildly, his green eyes intent on her confused face.

'I didn't say that.' Rosa's cheeks turned pink.

'As good as. I seem to remember you asking me if it was even civilised.'

'That was before I'd seen it,' Rosa protested defensively. 'Anyway, that's not why I'm here.'

'I didn't think so.' Liam leaned back, resting his right ankle across his left knee. 'Sam told me you'd wanted to speak to me before you left on Tuesday morning.'

Rosa stiffened. 'But you didn't consider it important enough to get in touch with me?' she exclaimed impulsively. 'Even though you're evidently much better now.'

'Oh, I am. Much better,' agreed Liam drily.

Rosa regarded him warily. 'So—were you going to get in touch with me or not?'

'Not,' he declared softly. 'I thought it was for the best.'

Rosa swallowed. 'Whose best? Yours, I suppose?'

'Mine, yes. And yours.' Liam watched her with unwilling interest. He didn't need this, he told himself, even as he added, 'I don't think we have anything more to say to one another, do you?'

'Well, obviously I do.' Rosa knew it would probably be wiser if she got to her feet and got out of here before she said or did something unforgivable. 'There's something else I want to ask you about Sophie.'

Her sister!

Liam only just prevented himself from using a word that wasn't acceptable in mixed company. But hadn't they dealt with her sister's disappearance to distraction already? He didn't even know the girl, but he disliked her intensely.

Dropping his foot to the floor, he leant forward, allowing his hands to hang free between his spread thighs. Then, in a controlled voice, he said, 'What about her?'

Rosa moistened dry lips. 'I—forgot to ask you if it was possible that a film was being made in another part of the Highlands.'

Liam turned his head to give her an incredulous look. 'Well, sure,' he said. 'People are always making films in this part of the world. So what? You think now that your sister might really have hooked up with a guy from a film production?'

'It's possible.' Despite the disbelieving look in Liam's eyes, Rosa knew a twinge of optimism. 'And I think you might have told me about the probabilities of these other productions.'

'Say what?' Liam was indignant. 'What the hell do they have to do with me?'

'Well, they're your books, aren't—?'

'Whoa!' Liam halted her there. 'You think I'm talking about an alternative production of one of *my* books?'

'Well, aren't you?'

'Hell, no.' Liam gave an exasperated snort. 'I was talking about films generally. For God's sake, if I'd thought they were making a film of one of mine elsewhere in the Highlands, don't you think I'd have told you?'

Rosa's shoulders sagged. 'So they're not?'

'No.'

'You're sure?'

Liam gave a half-laugh. 'Well, let's put it this way, I've signed no contracts.'

'You mean they haven't paid you?'

'If you want to put it like that.'

Rosa gave a heavy sigh. 'What other way is there? I'm sorry I've wasted your time.'

'Hey, don't say that.' As suddenly as before, Liam changed his mind about her. 'You've certainly provided a pleasant distraction on a particularly dull day.'

'I'm glad I've amused you.'

Rosa's voice was thick, but when she would have pushed to her feet Liam's hand on her thigh prevented her from rising. 'Don't go,' he said, his fingers registering the warmth of her flesh beneath the fine wool trousers. She was quivering, and when her eyes widened uncertainly, he added swiftly, 'Mrs Wilson is bringing us some coffee.'

Rosa's mouth was dry. But, in spite of everything, she knew that this was really why she'd come here. Oh, she'd wanted to ask him about Sophie, too. But she hadn't held out much hope in that regard. What she'd needed to know was if the instant attraction she'd felt between them was just a figment of her imagination.

It didn't feel like it at this moment. The fingers gripping her leg were both strong and oddly possessive. And when she lifted her head and looked into his eyes she saw a reflection of her own thwarted desires.

Dear heaven, she thought incredulously, he *did* want her.

She just wished she had the first idea of what she was going to do about it.

The knock at the door was timely. Liam released Rosa at once, rising to his feet as the housekeeper obeyed his summons and came into the room carrying a tray.

'Sam said you wanted coffee, Mr Jameson,' Mrs Wilson murmured, her gaze flickering quickly over his guest's bent head. 'Where would you like it?'

Liam's lips twitched a little at the woman's unknowing innuendo, but he gestured towards the low table that was set between the two sofas. 'Just here's fine,' he said, wondering if her interruption was fate, trying to bring him to his senses. Mrs Wilson set down the tray and straightened. 'Thanks.'

The door closed behind the housekeeper with a definite click, and, because anything else would have looked strange, Liam subsided again onto the sofa beside Rosa. But he avoided looking at her, saying instead, 'Help yourself.'

Rosa made no move to do so. She merely stared at the tray as if it might provide the answers she sought. A steaming jug of coffee, two porcelain cups, a cream jug and a sugar basin. Such ordinary items, yet they represented the difference between an increasing awareness and the coolness she now felt from Liam.

'I'm not thirsty,' she said at last. 'And I think I'd better go, after all.'

Liam's jaw clenched, and before he could prevent himself he asked, 'Do you want to?'

No!

Rosa turned her head. 'I don't know,' she said weakly.

Liam groaned, and, forgetting what he'd told himself since the moment he'd laid eyes on her, reached out and slipped his hand behind her nape. Then, before he could change his mind, he pulled her towards him.

And she came, seemingly willingly, her lips parting beneath his with a sensuality he hadn't expected. He'd intended to keep this light, inconsequential, but when her mouth opened he plunged his tongue into that wet, heated cavern without giving himself time to think.

She tasted hot and sweet and immensely desirable. Before he knew what he was doing, his hand had slid from her neck to the sensitive hollow of her spine. She arched towards him and he felt her taut breasts nudging his chest. And, God help him, his hand slipped lower, cupping the provocative curve of her bottom.

She jerked uncontrollably, but she didn't draw away, and he urged her back against the cushions behind her. He was kissing her now with a wild abandon that he hadn't felt since who knew when. If he'd *ever* felt this way, he conceded with unwilling honesty, as he ravaged her mouth again and again.

But this was not what he'd intended, he thought, in a rare moment of coherency. Not what he'd intended at all. He didn't indulge in one-night-stands with needy divorcees who were looking for no-strings sex. Besides, he hardly knew her. And she knew nothing of the monstrous scars that lurked beneath the expensive civility of his clothes. Hadn't he learned to his cost that women were not to be trusted? If he didn't want to scare her half to death, he should stop this. Now.

Rosa, however, knew nothing of his private misgivings. And, while she doubted anything lasting could come of it, she was ready and willing to take whatever Liam had to give. Her marriage to Colin, the pain she'd suffered when she'd discovered he'd been cheating on her, seemed a distant memory. Colin had never made her feel like this. Their relationship had been one of convenience, she realised, not passion.

She moved, slipping her hands about his neck, letting her fingers curl in the hair at his nape. His hair was only lightly tinged with grey, but thick, and virile. Like the rest of him, she thought a little breathlessly, feeling the unmistakable pressure of his arousal against her stomach.

The fight Liam was waging against his own needs was rapidly fading. When her tongue came to twine with his, he felt the blood thundering through his veins. He sucked on her lips, bit her tongue, felt his head spinning with the gnawing hunger inside him. He wanted her, he thought savagely. He wanted to bury his aching shaft in her wet heat.

His hand stroked her jawline, and when he lifted his mouth to take a breath his thumb brushed sensuously across her swollen lips. Her tongue appeared, laving his thumb as he bent to bite her earlobe, and he felt his arousal straining at his zip.

Her hair had come loose during their lovemaking, and he couldn't resist twining the fiery strands around his fingers. He brought them to her lips and kissed her through the silky curtain, heard her give a moan of ecstasy as he did so.

God, this was getting heavy, he thought, dragging his hand away—but only as far as her chest. He couldn't resist cupping her breast through her sweater, but when he bent to take one hard nipple into his mouth she shook her head and guided his hand to the hem of the jersey.

Beneath the woollen garment her skin was smooth and unblemished. Unlike his own, he thought bitterly. When he peeled the sweater up to her chin, he found pert breasts, almost bursting out of her half-bra. The sight of all that creamy flesh was a harsh reminder of his own scarred torso, and with a groan of anguish he buried his face between her breasts and said hoarsely, 'I can't do this!'

Rosa was breathing rapidly, her chest rising and falling swiftly, matching the sexual cravings he was inspiring in her. There was a wetness between her legs, and a pain stirring deep in her belly. As well as electric shocks that sparked along her nerves and left her aching, restive and wanting.

'You want me,' she protested, not knowing where she found the courage to say such a thing to him. God, only a few days ago she'd been convinced he could never be attracted to her. Yet here she was, telling him he wanted her, when he might easily be playing her along.

However, he didn't deny it. 'That doesn't matter,' Liam declared grimly, but when he put his hands on the cushions at either side of her head to lever himself away from her she wouldn't let him go.

'It *does* matter,' she insisted, cupping his face in her hands and forcing him to look at her. 'I'm not expecting a lifelong commitment here. I just want to—be with you. Is that so wrong?'

Liam groaned. 'It's not wrong—'

'Well, then?'

'You don't understand,' he muttered, and this time he succeeded in pulling away from her. He drew her sweater down again, hiding those luscious breasts from his hungry gaze. 'I'm not what you think.'

Rosa gazed at him, narrow-eyed. 'If you're going to tell me you're not normal, then—'

'I'm not a vampire,' Liam assured her harshly. 'But just take my word for it. This would never work.'

'It doesn't have to work.' Rosa struggled into a sitting position and stared at him appealingly. 'I like you, Liam. I have ever since you spoke to me on the ferry. I know I'm not sophisticated or glamorous, but I thought—I really thought you liked me, too.'

'I *do* like you,' muttered Liam savagely. 'This has nothing to do with liking or disliking you. It has to do with me. Only me!'

Rosa knew when she was beaten. She'd given it her best and Liam had shot her down in flames. She didn't know what was going on here, but she didn't believe half of what he was saying. For some reason he'd changed his mind about her.

Was he afraid she might expect something he couldn't give? Even now? Hurting, she had to deliver one final taunt—if only to salvage something from the wreck of her self-respect. 'It's *always* about you, isn't it, *Mr* Jameson?' she demanded, wrapping her arms about her suddenly chilled body. 'You're completely self-motivated, aren't you? Self first, self last, self everything!'

The injustice of that statement almost choked him. He'd been thinking of *her*, for God's sake! And of himself, too, he admitted, and how he'd feel when she saw him and turned away. But mostly of her, mostly to spare her the ugly patchwork his attacker had made of his body. It wouldn't occur to her that the reason he wore long-sleeved shirts and sweaters was because the man had almost chopped his arms to shreds.

Realising he would regret this, he got to his feet and faced her. Then, as she gazed up at him in sudden alarm, he tore his shirt open. Buttons popped and danced across the floor, and he realised he'd probably torn them off. But he didn't care. In that moment all he wanted to do was show her the proof of what he'd been saying.

Rosa got to her feet as he dragged the shirt off his shoulders, her breath catching in her throat when she saw the scars on his arms and chest. Someone had attacked him—with a knife, she guessed—and he'd raised his arms to defend himself.

So this was what he'd been hiding, she thought, wondering if he thought they detracted from him as a man. The scars were old, and in many cases fading. But the memories they'd left with him were still strong enough to tear him apart.

Oh, Lord, she fretted, ashamed that she'd made him do this. Not to mention accusing him of having lived a charmed life. But did he really think she'd be repulsed by his appearance? For heaven's sake, she was ashamed of *herself*, not him.

'I—I didn't know,' she began, wanting to reassure him. 'I'm sorry, Liam, I—'

'Not half as sorry as I am, believe me,' he snarled harshly. 'But, as you say, you didn't know. I suppose that's some excuse.' He snatched up his shirt and shoved his arms into the sleeves. 'But now you do, and I want you to go. I'll get Sam to show you out.'

'But, Liam—'

'Don't,' he said, limping heavily to the door. 'Believe me, I've had all the sympathy I can take.'

Rosa fretted about what had happened all the way back to the guesthouse. She didn't think about the rain, or the fact that the roads were slippy and she had to be careful she didn't skid into a bog. Her own safety meant nothing to her at that moment. She didn't even notice the stiffness of the steering wheel. All she could think about was Liam's face when he'd wrenched off his shirt and shown her those awful scars. She didn't think she'd ever forget the torment in his eyes.

It was only when she pulled up outside the guesthouse that she realised it had actually stopped raining. Even the wind seemed to have eased a little, and she could actually walk up the path to the door without getting blown off her feet.

Conversely, the knowledge that the storm was waning didn't cheer her up. The ferry would come and she'd leave the island. She'd never see Liam again.

'Is everything all right?' Mrs Ferguson met her in the hallway of the guesthouse, her brow creasing when she saw how drawn Rosa looked.

'Yes. Yes, everything's fine,' lied Rosa, knowing she couldn't discuss what had happened with anyone. 'Thank you for the use of your car. I must pay for the petrol, though.'

'Och, that's not necessary.' Mrs Ferguson clicked her tongue dismissively. 'I don't want anything for the tiny drop of fuel you'll have used. Like I said before you left, it will have done the vehicle good to have an outing. When my husband was alive he used to like to go bird-watching all over the island, but since he died I've scarcely had a use for it.'

'You're very kind.' Rosa forced a smile. 'It—er—it seems to be brightening up.'

'Yes, I thought so myself,' agreed the landlady, glancing out of the door. 'But you're looking a little peaked, Miss Chantry, if you don't mind my saying so. Are you sure you didn't find the journey too tiring?'

Tiring!

Rosa stifled the sob that rose in the back of her throat.

'Just—a bit,' she said, hoping that would satisfy the woman. 'I'm used to power steering, you see.'

'Power steering?' Mrs Ferguson sounded impressed. 'And what would that be when it's at home?'

'Oh—' Rosa wished she hadn't said anything. 'It just makes it easier to steer,' she explained, without elaborating, and with that she headed towards the stairs that led to her room.

CHAPTER TEN

THE REST OF THE DAY was an anticlimax.

After refusing Mrs Ferguson's offer of lunch, Rosa holed up in her room, wondering if she'd ever feel normal again. The events of the morning seemed unbelievable in retrospect. Had she really almost been seduced by a man against his will?

She simply wasn't the kind of woman things like that happened to. Her marriage to Colin Vincent and his subsequent betrayal had left her distinctly suspicious where men were concerned. Yet from the beginning she'd not had that feeling with Liam. Perhaps because she'd never expected that he might be attracted to her.

Even now, she hardly knew what he felt about her. Not enough to trust her, she acknowledged, wishing she'd had a chance to convince him she didn't care about his scars. Were they the reason he lived here, miles from any of the people he worked with? She wished she knew him better, wished she could show him that she—

She—what?

Rosa shivered. What was she thinking? She wasn't in love with him, for heaven's sake. In lust, maybe, and she very much regretted the way she'd had to leave the castle.

But she hardly knew the man. Certainly not enough to trust him with her love.

Nevertheless, that didn't stop her from regretting what had happened. She still didn't know what he thought of her—if he imagined she was used to doing that sort of thing.

She wasn't.

Rosa quivered. She couldn't ever remember behaving so shamelessly before, even with Colin. But then, the feelings she'd had for Colin had been nothing like this, and that was something else she regretted.

But had she really *asked* Liam to have sex with her? Had she really promised him there need be no commitment on his part, other than to take her to bed and make mad, passionate love to her?

Her face burned at the memory. Burned, too, at the realisation that she'd meant it. That she meant it still. She wanted him. Wanted to be with him. And something told her it would have been an experience she would never forget.

But it wasn't going to happen. Liam had made sure of that. In one devastating move he'd shown her exactly how damaged he was. Not just physically. His physical scars had healed. It was the other scars he carried beneath the surface that worried Rosa.

Because it was that sensitivity, which seemed to be as raw now as when the attack had happened, that had caused him to turn away from her. She was no psychologist, but she'd gamble that someone else was responsible for the protective shell he'd built around himself. Someone had hurt him, and she didn't believe it was his attacker.

So who? It had to be a woman, she decided painfully. A special woman. A woman he'd been in love with. Someone he'd been relying on to support him through his ordeal…

The phone rang downstairs and Rosa tensed. Not that she expected it to be for her. Liam wasn't likely to try and get in touch with her again.

Nevertheless, her heart leapt when Mrs Ferguson called, 'It's for you, Miss Chantry.' And then sank again when she added, 'It's your mother.'

What now?

Rosa felt the weight of her own inadequacy descend on her as she hurried down the stairs to take the call. Yes, she'd asked Liam about the film, she rehearsed silently. But, no, she had no further news to give her mother.

'Hello, Mum,' she said, picking up the receiver, injecting a note of optimism into her voice. 'You'll be pleased to hear the storm's over at last. I'll be leaving the island on Monday at the latest.'

'Will you, dear?' Mrs Chantry sounded strangely agitated. 'Well, that's good.' She paused. 'Will you come straight home?'

Rosa frowned. 'I thought I might contact an information centre on the mainland and find out if they know—'

'Sophie's not in Scotland,' broke in her mother swiftly. And then, before Rosa could object, she added, 'She's been in London, but she's home now.'

Rosa was stunned. 'In London?' she echoed, blankly.

'Yes.' Her mother didn't sound as if she was enjoying this. 'She's been with some man she met at the pop festival. Some musician, I believe.'

'You're not serious!'

'I am.' Mrs Chantry sighed. 'I'm sorry, Rosa.'

'But why did she tell Mark she was going to Scotland?'

'I don't know.' Clearly her mother would have preferred not to go on with this. 'To put us off the scent, I suppose.

She knew I'd have worried if I'd known she was with some guitarist with a pop group. What with all the drug-taking that goes on and—'

'But you *were* worried, Mum,' Rosa reminded her. 'My God, when you rang me last Saturday night you were practically hysterical.'

'Oh, I wasn't, Rosa. You're exaggerating. Good heavens, we all know what Sophie's like. She's so impetuous!'

'So irresponsible,' muttered Rosa darkly. 'Is she there? Put her on. I want to speak to her.'

'You can't.' Before Rosa could argue, Mrs Chantry explained her reasons. 'Mark called a little while ago, and she's gone round to his house to try and patch things up with him.'

'Well, he's a fool if he believes anything she tells him,' said Rosa irritably. For heaven's sake, was she the only one in the family with a lick of sense? 'I can't believe you're letting her get away with this. If it had been me at her age, I'd have been grounded for a month!'

'Well, it's no good me going on at her, Rosa,' declared Mrs Chantry unhappily. 'She's going away to university soon enough, and if I play the heavy she's not going to want to come home at all.'

'Oh, Mum!' Rosa groaned. 'You can't let her blackmail you. She ran off with a musician, a man she'd only just met, who she knew nothing about. He could have been a—a white slaver for all she knew.'

'Oh, Rosa.' Mrs Chantry gave a little laugh now. 'White slaver, indeed!' She waited a beat, and when Rosa didn't say anything she added firmly, 'Anyway, she's learned her lesson. She says he dumped her when she refused to go to bed with him.'

And believe that if you will, thought Rosa cynically. But all she said was, 'Did she tell you why she went with him in the first place?'

'Oh, apparently he said he could introduce her to some people he knew in television,' said her mother, relaxing a little now that she'd delivered her news. 'She shouldn't have believed him. I told her that.'

'And where did Liam Jameson come in?' asked Rosa shortly. 'Or hasn't she told you that?'

Her mother hesitated. 'Oh—well, that might have been my fault.'

'Your fault?' Rosa was confused. 'How could it be your fault?'

'Well...' Mrs Chantry was obviously searching for words. 'I evidently jumped to the wrong conclusion.'

'I don't understand.'

'No.' Her mother sighed. 'No, you wouldn't.' There was another pause, and then she said reluctantly, 'Well, you know how much Sophie likes Liam Jameson's books?'

'Yes.'

'And how she'd said how great it would be to star in one of his films?'

'You're kidding!'

'No. No, I'm not.' Mrs Chantry spoke indignantly. 'She has said that. Heaps of times. And—and when Mark rang and said she'd run off to Scotland with some man she'd met at the pop festival—'

Rosa groaned. 'I don't believe this!'

'It—it's true.' Her mother sniffed pathetically. 'Mark did say that she'd told him that this man was going to introduce her to all the right people, and—'

'And you put two and two together and made fifteen,'

said Rosa shortly. 'Mum, why didn't you tell me this before I left?'

'Would you have gone if I had?'

No!

Rosa blew out a breath. 'Possibly not.'

'Probably not,' declared her mother tersely. 'I know you, Rosa. If you'd thought I was just clutching at straws, you'd never have approached Liam Jameson.'

And wasn't that the truth? thought Rosa, an unpleasant little pain making itself felt in her temple. 'Oh, Mum,' she said wearily, 'I wish you'd told me just the same.'

'And have you tell me what a stupid woman I am?' demanded Mrs Chantry. 'I thought you'd be glad to hear your sister was home, safe and sound. Instead all you can do is grumble about both of us!'

Rosa knew it was ridiculous. She was thirty-two, for goodness' sake. But her eyes filled with tears at her mother's harsh words. They were so unjustified, so unfair. She hadn't complained, not really. But Sophie was totally selfish and her mother refused to see it.

'I'd better go,' she said, hoping the catch in her voice wasn't audible to anyone else. 'Mrs Ferguson's probably waiting to use the phone.'

Which was unlikely, she conceded. Apart from this call, the phone hadn't rung at all while she'd been in the guest-house. Evidently people in Kilfoil tended to do their gossiping face to face.

'All right.' If Mrs Chantry suspected that the reason Rosa was ending the call was because she'd been a little unkind, she wasn't prepared to admit it. 'I'll expect you when I see you, then. Take care.'

'Bye.'

Rosa replaced the handset and scrubbed an impatient hand across her eyes. She was not going to cry, she told herself, even if the day had just gone from bad to worse. She had to focus on the future, on getting home to her little flat in Ripon, which suddenly seemed very far away. School would be starting again in a couple of weeks, and she had lessons to prepare before then.

Liam always stayed at the Moriarty Hotel when he was in London. It was a small, select establishment, known to only a few people, and they, like himself, reserved a suite of rooms year round, so that it was always available whenever it was needed.

It was one of the perks of being successful, he thought, as he drove south on the motorway. He could stay there completely anonymously, which suited him very well.

Not that he intended staying more than a couple of nights there on this visit. He was due to spend a few days at the Erskine Clinic in Knightsbridge, undergoing some further therapy on his leg.

Ever since August, when he'd been caught out in the storm because of the dogs, he'd been having an increasing amount of discomfort in his thigh. The local doctor thought he might have torn a ligament, and rather than wait for it to get better, which might not happen, Liam had been forced to seek relief.

Of course Sam thought he was crazy, driving to London. His opinion was that Liam should have used the helicopter. But helicopters tended to advertise one's arrival, and that was the last thing Liam wanted to do.

He'd left Scotland behind a little while ago, and now he was some miles beyond Penrith, heading towards the service area at Tebay. He might stop there, he reflected. He could do with a cup of coffee and the opportunity to stretch his legs. And to look at the map, he conceded, not prepared to consider why he should need to do so. His route was familiar enough, goodness knew. South on the M6 as far as the M5. then east on the M40 until he reached the outskirts of London. What could be simpler?

He parked near the service buildings at Tebay and went inside to use the facilities and buy a coffee. Then he carried it back to the car and pulled his map out of the glove locker.

Less than a mile farther on there was a turn-off for Scotch Corner. Well, for Kirby Stephen initially, but it eventually intersected with the A66 east, which in turn intersected with the A1 at Scotch Corner. And about twenty miles south of Scotch Corner was the small Yorkshire market town of Ripon.

Ripon!

Liam swallowed a mouthful of his coffee, wincing at its bitter taste. Now, why would he want to know how to get to Ripon? Okay, he'd found out from Mrs Ferguson that that was where Rosa Chantry lived, but so what? It was nearly two months since he'd seen her, and after the way he'd behaved he doubted very much whether she'd want to see him again.

He didn't even know why he was still thinking about her. He was too old to believe that their association had been anything more than a brief infatuation with sex. He'd wanted her, yes, but experience had taught him that you didn't always get what you wanted. There was no doubt that she'd been horrified when she'd glimpsed the ugly patchwork beneath his shirt. And she hadn't even seen the worst of it. It was a mercy he could still function as a man.

He tried to excuse his interest by telling himself he was concerned about her. Had she found her sister yet? Was she safe and well? Surely she must be. Despite searching the Internet, scanning every newspaper published in the Ripon area, he'd never read anything about a Sophie Chantry being missing. Wherever she was, she wasn't making news, and that was usually a good sign.

For Rosa's sake, he hoped so. He couldn't believe that in this day and age, with all the publicity there was about the dangers of young girls going off with men they knew nothing about, her sister should have behaved so foolishly. She was either completely naïve or completely stupid. Remembering what Rosa had told him, he'd put his money on the latter.

He folded the map and put it back in the glove box, and then sat for a while drinking his coffee. What now? Was he going to get back on the motorway and drive directly to London, as he'd told Sam? Or was he going to make a detour to the north-east?

He considered. A glance at his watch told him it was three o'clock on a Tuesday afternoon in October. By his reckoning, it would be five o'clock before he reached Ripon, if that was where he intended to go. How did he know she'd be home from work? Or even alone? Was he willing to take the risk just to satisfy a whim he'd probably regret later? He knew the answer, and he tossed the empty cup into a rubbish bin. If he didn't see Rosa again he'd never know how he really felt.

Happily, traffic was fairly light, and he arrived at the out-skirts of Ripon soon after a quarter to five. There were plenty of cars heading out of town—probably commuters, making their way home, he decided. Now all he had to do was find someone who could tell him where Richmond Road was.

A policeman was patrolling the narrow street beside the cathedral, and although there were yellow lines warning him not to stop Liam pulled in beside him. Lowering the nearside window, he leant across the seat. 'I'm looking for Richmond Road,' he said ruefully. 'You couldn't help me, could you?'

The policeman looked as if he was about to point out that this was a no waiting area, but then seemed to take pity on him. 'Richmond Road,' he said thoughtfully. 'Yes.' He turned. 'You've just come past it. It's that way, just off Winston Street.'

Liam stifled a curse. This was a one-way street, and he'd already discovered that the town centre was a maze of similar thoroughfares. How the hell was he supposed to retrace his steps?

'It might be easier if you parked and walked back,' suggested the policemen, apparently aware of his dilemma. 'I could give you directions, but at this time of the afternoon—'

'I understand.'

Liam gave a brief nod and rolled up the window again. Was he being a damn fool? he wondered, driving back into the market square. All this fuss, just to find a woman who might not even be willing to speak to him. He dreaded to think what Sam would say if he found out.

He eventually found a car park just off the market square. And, because most people were heading home, he had no problem in finding a space. Then, hauling his woollen overcoat out of the back seat, he locked the car and pocketed the keys, pushing his hands deep into his coat pockets as he trudged back towards the cathedral.

A bell tolled and he realised it was already half-past five.

It had taken him longer to find her house than to drive from Scotch Corner to Ripon. And he still had about a five-hour journey ahead of him, if he was planning to reach London tonight.

Fortunately, it was a dry evening, though it was cold. The wind swept along these narrow streets, and his hip and leg became stiff and taut with pain. He should have stayed with the car, he thought. Walking any distance in his present state was madness. And all to see a woman he barely knew.

He found Richmond Road without much difficulty. It was a street of semi-detached houses, and it was still light enough for him to see number 24. He glanced at the note he'd stuffed in his pocket. It said number 24b. But there was no 24b. No 24a, either. Had she given Mrs Ferguson a false address?

He frowned. Then, deciding the only thing he could do was knock at number 24 and ask for directions again, he opened the front gate and walked up the path. That was when he saw the intercom pinned to the wall beside the door. It had been too dark for him to see it before. Evidently 24b was an apartment; likewise 24a.

He cast a glance at the windows. There were lights upstairs, so someone was home. But was that apartment 24a or 24b? He wouldn't know until he rang the bell.

'Yes?'

The voice that answered his summons was unmistakable. Liam disliked the way it danced along his nerves and curled its way around his heart. For God's sake, what was the matter with him? Even Kayla had never made him feel like this.

'Rosa?' His voice was a little hoarse suddenly. 'It's me, Liam Jameson. May I come up?'

Silence. Liam wondered what he'd do if she refused to speak to him. Break down the door? Walk away? He hoped he didn't have to make that decision.

'Push the door,' she said at last, and with a feeling of relief he heard the sound of the buzzer that released the latch.

Inside it was dark. He could just make out a hallway, leading to the back of the house, and a flight of stairs to the first floor.

As if she thought he might have some doubts about which apartment was hers, a light suddenly shone down from the top of the stairs. Rosa was standing on the landing above, looking down at him, and with a deep intake of air he closed the door and started up.

She looked different, he thought, and then realised she'd had her hair cut. Now it swung about her shoulders, still a fiery mass of curls, but softer, more feminine. She was wearing loose-fitting black trousers and a green blouse of some silky material that tipped off one shoulder as she moved. She looked good, he thought grimly. Too good to be spending the evening watching the television. Alone.

His leg stiffened as he mounted the stairs, and for a moment he couldn't move. Hoping she wouldn't notice, he said tightly, 'Sorry if I'm intruding.'

Rosa frowned, and he was almost sure she was going to comment on his momentary paralysis. But then he was able to move his leg again, and she stepped back into the lighted doorway behind her. 'You're not intruding. Come in.'

CHAPTER ELEVEN

'THANKS.'

Liam was very relieved to reach the landing. He didn't think he could have climbed another step, and he was already wondering how the hell he was going to get back to where he'd left his car. Perhaps he could call a cab? One thing was for sure: he didn't think he could walk all that way again tonight.

Meanwhile, Rosa was wondering what he was doing here. She tried to tell herself it could have nothing to do with what had happened before she left the castle, yet what else could it be?

He must have got her address from Mrs Ferguson. She could imagine that lady's surprise at such a request. She must have wondered why he hadn't contacted his publisher. Unless, for some reason, he'd told her the truth.

Her eyes darted about the room as he entered, trying to see it through his eyes. It was a comfortable room, a through dining and sitting room combined. But it was shabby, and nothing like the luxurious apartments he was used to.

She snatched up a discarded pair of tights she'd left draped over one of the dining chairs, and removed a magazine from the chenille couch. 'Why don't you sit down?'

she invited, aware of the laboured way he'd climbed the stairs. 'You look—tired.'

'Don't you mean beat?' suggested Liam drily, but he did subside onto the couch with some relief. 'I'm a bit stiff, that's all. I've been driving since early this morning.'

Rosa's eyes widened. 'But it's Tuesday!'

'So?'

'I thought the ferry only ran on Mondays and Thursdays.' She shook her head. 'Oh, of course. You probably used your helicopter?'

Liam slanted a glance up at her. 'How did you know I had a helicopter?'

Rosa straightened. 'Mrs Ferguson told me.' She paused. 'When—when I was stranded on the island, she suggested asking you if you could help.'

'Ah.' Liam nodded. 'The kindly Mrs Ferguson.' He shrugged. 'Well, I'm sorry to disappoint you, but I spent last night at Jack Macleod's.'

'Who?' Rosa had never heard of Jack Macleod.

'The man you saw me talking to that morning we took the ferry to Kilfoil,' he reminded her, resting back against the cushions and pushing his hands into the pockets of his coat. 'Or am I the only one who remembers that?'

Rosa moistened her lips. 'No. No, I remember,' she said defensively. 'Is he a friend of yours?'

'A good friend,' agreed Liam. 'He lives in Mallaig, and when I first bought the island he offered to put me in touch with the people I needed to renovate the castle and the cottages. His grandparents used to live on Kilfoil, and he was a great help. We've remained friends ever since.'

'Oh, I see.' Rosa absorbed this. Then, 'I suppose Mrs Ferguson gave you my address?'

'She did.' Liam regarded her from beneath lashes any woman would have died for. 'I hope you don't mind.'

'Why should I mind?' Rosa realised she was still holding the magazine and the tights she'd picked up when he arrived. With an absent gesture, she crossed the room to dispose of them into a drawer before turning down the gas fire. The room seemed overly hot suddenly, and with her back to him she added, 'Can I get you anything? A drink?'

'A beer would be good,' he said, not really wanting anything at this moment. The pain in his leg was just beginning to subside, and the last thing he wanted was to have to walk on it again. 'Um—did you find your sister?'

Rosa straightened and turned to him, the blouse sliding off her shoulder again to reveal the black strap of her bra. 'She was here when I got back,' she confessed wryly. 'She'd been in London all along.'

'London?' Liam was briefly diverted. 'What the hell was she doing in London?'

'Making out with a musician she met at the pop festival,' replied Rosa, with a grimace. 'He apparently dumped her when she refused to sleep with him.'

Liam looked doubtful at this, and Rosa had to continue. 'I know. Incredible, isn't it? But my mother believes everything she says.' She sighed. 'Sophie can wrap her round her little finger.'

Liam stared at her. 'So where did I come in?'

'Oh—' Rosa's cheeks reddened. 'That was my mother's fault. When Mark—he's Sophie's boyfriend—phoned her to tell her Sophie had gone to Scotland with some man who was going to help her get into the movies, she immediately thought of you.'

'Why, for God's sake?'

'Well, like I told you, Sophie's always been such a fan of yours. I suppose she needed something to focus on, and you were it.'

'So it was your mother who sent you to Kilfoil?'

'Mmm.' Rosa nodded. 'But Sophie had said she was going to Scotland. That part was true.'

Liam shook his head in disbelief. 'Dare I ask why?'

'To put us off the scent?' Rosa shrugged. 'Looking back, I must have been a fool to believe anything my mother said. But she is half Italian, and she was practically hysterical when she phoned me.' She pulled a rueful face. 'Now—a beer.' She started towards the kitchen. 'Is that all?'

Not nearly, thought Liam, but he assured her that it was, watching as she went into the adjoining room. She walked quickly, and he realised she was nervous. He wondered why. Was she expecting someone else. A man, maybe?

That thought irritated him beyond reason. God, he couldn't believe how much he'd wanted to see her again. It added to the sense of impatience he was feeling at his own weakness. Dammit, he hadn't come here for her sympathy. He'd wanted to test her, but not in this way.

Gritting his teeth, he hauled himself to his feet again and made his way across the floor to the open doorway. Then, propping his shoulder against the jamb, he said, 'Do you live alone?'

Rosa jumped. Having acknowledged how tired he was, she'd expected him to stay on the couch. She'd already extracted a bottle of beer from the fridge, and had been about to decant it into a glass, but his appearance had startled her.

'Um—yes,' she said, concentrating on unscrewing the cap. However, when she would have poured it into the tumbler she'd taken from the cupboard, Liam stopped her.

'It's okay,' he said. 'I'll drink it from the bottle.'

Rosa looked doubtful. 'Are you sure?'

'I'm sure,' he said, holding out his hand, and with a shrug she passed the bottle to him.

He didn't move from the doorway, however, and she found herself watching as he carried the bottle to his lips and took a hearty swallow.

The muscles in his throat moved as he drank, the mark she'd seen when she was at the castle the only pale scar on flesh that was both brown and supple. And, just watching him, she felt again the flicker of desire—of awareness—that had been so unfamiliar to her until she'd met him.

Liam lowered the bottle suddenly, and turned to look at her. And, just like that, her limbs turned to jelly. It took an actual physical effort to look away from those jade-green eyes and say, albeit a little breathlessly, 'Why don't you go and sit down again? You can't enjoy anything standing up.'

'Don't you believe it,' said Liam provocatively, setting the bottle down on the unit beside him and holding out his hand. 'Come here.'

Rosa swallowed. 'Do you need some help getting—'

'No!' he exploded angrily. 'I don't need your help. Not in that way, anyway.' He gave her an exasperated look. 'Just come here, will you?'

Rosa hesitated, but eventually she left the support of the fridge behind and approached him. 'Now what?'

'Like you don't know,' he retorted softly, catching her wrist and bringing its sensitive network of veins to his mouth. 'Kiss me.'

Rosa's breathing faltered. 'Liam—'

'Just do it, dammit,' he demanded harshly, and without

another word she stepped closer and reached up to brush his lips with hers.

Liam gave a frustrated snort. 'Is that the best you can do?' He used his free hand to trace the shape of her jawline, allowing his fingers to move into the fiery glory of her hair. 'Kiss me, Rosa. Like you mean it. I didn't drive all this way just so you could give me a beer.'

'So why did you?' Rosa looked up into his strong face, resisting the urge to brush her own fingers across his lips. 'Drive all this way, I mean?'

Liam's eyes narrowed. 'Guess.'

Rosa took a breath. 'Because you wanted to see me?'

Liam's expression was sardonic. 'Gee, you have a real way with words.'

'So you tell me what to say,' she exclaimed, at once defensive and excited. 'Why did you want to see me? As I recall it, you couldn't wait to get rid of me before.'

'Yeah.' Liam made a mocking sound. 'That's what I let you think, didn't I?'

'Wasn't it true?'

'Hell, yes, it was true.' He tugged gently at a handful of hair. 'It's still true.' He grimaced. 'But I find I'm not quite as heroic as I thought I was.'

'Heroic?' Rosa was puzzled.

Liam sighed, shifting his weight from one foot to the other. 'If I had any sense at all, I wouldn't be here.'

Rosa drew back. 'Well, if you feel like that—' she began, only to break off in surprise when he bent and covered her mouth with his.

It wasn't totally unexpected. Goodness, they'd been edging towards this moment since she'd opened the door. But even Rosa was unprepared for the urgency with which he pulled her closer, and the groan that emanated from deep in his throat when he did so.

Her lips parted of their own accord, and Liam's tongue swept eagerly into her mouth. He found he wasn't immune to the temptation posed by her soft and yielding body pressed against his, or ashamed to take advantage of her obvious weakness. This was what he'd wanted since she'd let him into the apartment, and although his thigh was aching, a much more urgent ache was developing between his legs.

The kiss lengthened and deepened, draining them with its urgency, leaving them both breathless and trembling. Trying to hang on to his sanity, Liam left her mouth to seek the pulse beating behind her ear, biting the lobe feverishly, finding it increasingly difficult to keep his head.

Her blouse slipped off her shoulder again, and this time Liam tipped the bra strap aside, too, so that he could nuzzle the creamy slopes of her breasts. He nipped her with his teeth, sucked hungrily on her soft flesh, took pleasure in seeing his mark on her.

'You want me,' she exclaimed unsteadily, reaching up to grab the hair at the back of his neck in an effort to ground herself. 'You really want me.'

'You noticed.' His voice was rough with emotion. 'Yeah, I want you. Are you going to tell me you don't feel the same?'

'That would be pretty stupid, wouldn't it?' Rosa replied huskily. 'I think you know how I feel, or you wouldn't be here.'

'I know how you *think* you feel,' he said in response. 'But you don't know everything.'

Rosa quivered, feeling the thick pressure of his arousal building against her abdomen. 'I have been married,' she reminded him gently, but Liam only snorted at her words.

'That's not what I meant and you know it,' he muttered, releasing himself abruptly and turning aside into the living room. Then, not facing her, he said, 'You're not going to be horrified if I take off my pants?'

Rosa went after him then, sliding her arms around him from behind and pressing her face against the soft wool of his overcoat. 'You flatter yourself,' she whispered, trying to make light of what he'd said, but Liam only uttered a rude word.

'You think you've seen the worst of it, but you haven't,' he said harshly. 'You've had time to get over what you saw, but there are other scars—'

'Shh!' Rosa let go of him to come round and face him. 'Stop talking like that.' She paused. 'If you'd given me a chance to speak that morning at the castle, I'd have told you then that I don't horrify that easily.'

'But you were shocked—'

'Of course I was.' Rosa was indignant. 'For heaven's sake, who wouldn't have been in my position? I'd had no idea—' She broke off, and then went on more steadily, 'But I wasn't—repelled, repulsed, whatever ugly ideas are buzzing around in that head of yours. I thought it was a shame, that's all. That someone could have been evil enough to do that to you. If I felt anything, it was compassion—'

'I don't need your—'

'But I guessed you'd probably had all the compassion you could stomach.' She overrode him grimly. 'Besides, you must know you have so much else going for you. But you didn't give me a chance to say anything except goodbye.'

Liam's shoulders sagged. 'I didn't think there was anything else to say.'

'I suppose that depends on what you're going to do

now,' she replied, looking up into his troubled features. 'Whether you're going to storm off into the night or—take off your coat.'

Liam gazed down at her. 'You know, I want to believe you mean this.'

'Then do it,' she exclaimed fiercely. 'Take off your coat.' She stepped forward and slid her hands beneath his coat, slipping it off his shoulders. 'You must be warm in here, with all these clothes on.'

'I am warm—hot, actually,' he muttered. 'But it has hell all to do with what I'm wearing.' He let the heavy overcoat fall to the floor. 'Come here.'

'No, you come here,' she said, taking his hand and leading him across the room. Another door opened into a short corridor with two doors leading from it. One, he guessed, led to a bathroom. The other had to be Rosa's bedroom.

He was right. The room she led him into was small, but attractive, with honey-coloured walls and a creamy shag carpet underfoot. There was a bed—a single, he noticed, with a satisfied curl of his lip—a wardrobe and a chest of drawers. The curtains, which matched the pale green coverlet, were drawn, and Rosa bent to switch on a lamp beside the bed.

'I know this is nothing like what you're used to—' she was beginning, but he swung her round to face him, taking her mouth again in a kiss that left them both hot and panting for breath.

'I want to get used to you, not this room,' Liam told her when he could speak again. 'But could we lose the lamp? I don't think I'm up to being inspected.'

Rosa wanted to tell him not to be silly, but she respected his feelings and obediently turned the lamp off again. 'Better?' she asked huskily, his large frame just a silhouette now in the light that filtered through from the living room.

'Much better,' he agreed, moving towards her, and she sank down onto the side of the bed, trying to draw him with her.

But Liam had other ideas. Ignoring the stiffness in his hip, he knelt in front of her, burying his face in the hollow between her breasts. 'Do you know how much I've wanted this?' he asked thickly, his hands slipping beneath the blouse at her waist. And then, more impatiently, 'How the hell do you take this thing off?'

'Let me,' said Rosa shakily, crossing her arms and pulling the offending garment over her head. 'It's easy when you know how.'

'Don't I know it?' said Liam, shoving his own jacket to the floor. His sweater followed it, but when he realised that only his shirt separated all her unblemished loveliness from his disfigured torso he paused. Then, in a strangled voice, he added, 'Are you really sure about this?'

'As sure as I've ever been about anything in my life,' Rosa assured him in a breathless voice. Her fingers started on the buttons of his shirt. 'Can I?'

Liam's breath caught in his throat. 'If you want to.'

'I want to,' she whispered, and moments later he felt the cool draught of air across his heated skin.

She leaned towards him, her lips finding the pattern of lines left by his injuries and tracing each one with her tongue. There was no revulsion, no aversion. Just tender contact with his skin.

It was his cue to urge her back against the mattress, covering her with his body, loosening the clasp of her bra and freeing the incredible warmth of her breasts against his chest. He couldn't resist taking one swollen nipple into his mouth, and she gave a little moan as he did so. He rolled the tight bud against his tongue and suckled greedily. Dear God, why had he stayed away so long?

She shifted restlessly beneath him, her fingers tangling in his hair as she arched her body towards his. And, although Liam would have liked to prolong this, he knew he wasn't going to be able to. Already his erection was threatening to burst out of his pants.

It had to be almost twenty-five years since he'd been in such a state of arousal, he thought incredulously. Not since he was a teenager had he ever been in danger of losing control—not just of his body but of his mind, too. The blood was thundering through his veins in anticipation of what he was going to do to her. He actually came out in a sweat at the thought of burying his shaft in her hot sheath.

He pushed his hand down between them and found the button at the waistband of her trousers. It opened easily, and with a shuddering breath he slipped his hand inside. Encountering lacy silk, he frowned, remembering how nervous she'd seemed earlier. The idea that she might have dressed for some other man caused his blood pressure to rise even more.

But he refused to ruin the beauty of this moment by allowing his own jealousy to destroy the mood. Instead, his hands moved beneath the lace and cupped her mound.

'That feels so good,' he whispered, one finger penetrating the silky curls of hair to find the swollen nubbin trapped within her folds and rubbing gently. 'I knew it would.'

'For me, too,' said Rosa hoarsely, her hands tangling with his as she struggled to loosen his trousers. 'Please,' she added brokenly. 'I want you inside me when I come.'

Liam's breathing faltered. The image her words was creating caused him to quicken his efforts to free her from the rest of her clothes, and pretty soon her trousers and the lace thong joined her blouse on the floor.

'Now you,' Rosa urged huskily, and with only a momentary hesitation Liam loosened his pants and shoved them down his legs.

Now Rosa could slip her hands into the waistband of his boxers, and she took full advantage. Her tantalising fingers shaped his butt, squeezing his cheeks, pressing his erection into the parted curve of her legs.

'Take these off, too,' she ordered him unsteadily, and, with her help, the boxers also found their way to the floor.

But when she would have taken him into her hands he stopped her. 'Give me a break,' he groaned, his action as much a need to protect his self-restraint as a desire to hide his scarred flesh a little longer. 'I'm only human.'

'I'm so glad,' she said, her breath catching in her throat, and in spite of his efforts to prevent it she managed to wrap her soft fingers around him. If she noticed the hard ridge of skin that arrowed down into his groin she didn't mention it, her soft caresses almost driving him over the edge. 'Luther Killian can't possibly be as sexy as you.'

Liam swallowed convulsively. 'What do *you* know about Luther Killian?' he asked thickly.

'Oh, I bought a book of yours in Scotland, and I've finally managed to read it.'

'Finally?'

Although he was aching to possess her, he forced himself to enjoy the foreplay, and she trembled beneath him. 'Mmm,' she said unsteadily. 'I couldn't read it when—when I was on the island. It reminded me too much of you.

But when I'd finally decided I was never going to see you again I thought it was the closest to you I was going to get.'

'Ah.' Liam released the breath he'd hardly been aware he was holding. 'And now?'

'And now I just want to do it with you,' she told him in a shaky voice. 'Please.'

CHAPTER TWELVE

LIAM REALISED he must have slept when he opened his eyes to find himself alone in the bed.

He hadn't been conscious of Rosa getting up. He hadn't been conscious of anything, really, since the shuddering climax of their lovemaking. Which was why he felt so relaxed, he supposed, so sated with pleasure. For a few moments he was content to just lie there and relive every minute of it.

He felt weak, thinking about what had happened. He'd known Rosa was responsive, but she'd completely overwhelmed him. She been so hot, so downright sexy, that he'd abandoned every inhibition he'd ever had.

He'd even forgotten why he'd been so apprehensive of making love with her. And if she'd been aware of any faults in his appearance she hadn't shown it. She'd actually made him believe in himself again, believe that he'd found a woman who saw the man and not the flaws.

He recalled the moment when he'd felt his erection tight against her vagina. Pushing into her that first time, he'd been half out of his mind with pleasure. She'd assured him there was no need for him to wear a condom, and the sensation of skin against skin had been a potent stimulant.

He'd been aware of Rosa holding her breath as he'd possessed her. 'Are you all right?' he'd asked roughly, hoping she wasn't about to bail on him, and Rosa had expelled a little sigh.

'I was just thinking how big you are,' she'd confessed, a catch in her voice.

'And that's a problem?'

'Not to me,' she'd responded at once. 'Maybe to you.'

'Oh, baby!' Liam's voice had revealed an uneven thread of humour. 'That's no problem. You're so hot, I feel as if I'm burning up!'

'And that's good?'

'That's very good,' he'd assured her fervently. 'Just don't expect me to wait too long.'

But when he'd finally penetrated her fully, he'd found he'd wanted to prolong it. With her tight around him, and her breasts crushed against his chest, he'd wanted it to last and last. It had felt so good to be a part of her, cradled deep within her. He'd usually found the anticipation so much better than the realisation, and he hadn't wanted anything to spoil something so beautiful.

But then Rosa had wound a slim leg about his, and caressed his calf with the sole of her foot. It had been such a simple thing—a sensual abrasion, that was all—but it had almost blown his mind. Every movement she'd made had aroused him further, and the urge to fulfil all the fantasies he'd had about her had instantly focussed on the heavy shaft in its tender sheath.

He'd begun to move then, slowly at first, testing the slick muscles that had expanded around him. There'd been a wilful pleasure in pulling back from her, almost to the point of withdrawal, and then thrusting in again, feeling the cravings he had build and build.

He couldn't remember when the mindless excitement of what he'd been doing had taken over. He just knew he'd quickened his pace to try and calm the feverish beating of his heart.

And Rosa had responded, moving with him, so that he'd felt the gathering momentum of her orgasm almost before she'd been aware of it herself.

Of course the sounds she'd made and the ripples of her climax had totally stoned him. His own release had followed close behind, and what had begun as a gentle supplication had quickly accelerated into a glorious abandonment to sensuality.

His own orgasm had seemed to last for ever. Long after he'd been sure he must have drained himself into her, he'd still been shaking in her arms. He'd never had an experience like it. All the doubts he'd had coming here, the tension he'd felt when he'd seen Rosa again, had all melted away. He knew he'd done the right thing by taking the detour, and he was fairly sure she felt the same.

But where was she? Easing himself up on one elbow, Liam tried to see his watch. What time was it? It was still dark outside, so it obviously wasn't morning. But how long had he slept?

The sound of a man's raised voice jarred him out of any sense of complacency. It came from the living room, and he realised he'd been hearing the buzz of voices for some time. He reached for the lamp and turned it on, pulling the sheet over his lower limbs as he did so. Just after 9:00 p.m. he saw with a frown. What the hell was it? Had Rosa got up and turned the television on?

He thought about calling her, but that seemed too presumptuous. He decided to wait until she came back before asking what was going on. And he knew she would, sooner or later. What they'd shared was not going to go away.

And then the man used Rosa's name.

'For God's sake, Rosa,' he exclaimed, his voice raised as before. 'I thought we were going to talk about this.'

Liam didn't hear Rosa's answer. She spoke in a much lower tone, and he wondered if that was because she was considering him. Or was it just that she didn't want him to hear what she was saying? Or know that she had another visitor? Maybe the one she'd dressed up for, he thought, with an uncontrollable spurt of jealousy.

Thrusting the covers aside, he swung his legs to the floor. Then, rescuing his boxers from where he'd tossed them, he pulled them on over his ankles before standing up. Thankfully, although his leg still ached, the rest had restored some strength to his muscles. If he had to walk back to his car tonight, he reckoned he could just about do it.

By the time he'd put on his jeans and shirt, the voices were barely audible. He pulled his sweater over his head and shouldered into the leather jacket, thinking that if he had to meet Rosa's visitor, whoever he was, he was going to be prepared.

The lamp gave off little illumination, so he took a chance and opened the door of the room across the hall. As he'd hoped, it was a bathroom, and he turned on the light and quickly ran a comb thorough his unruly hair.

He was hungry, he thought, coming out of the bathroom again. Bloody hungry. He'd forgotten good sex could do that for you: first the senses, then the stomach. Perhaps they could send out for a pizza, he thought, his mouth already watering at the prospect of melted mozzarella. Then—well, then the possibilities were endless.

He was about to enter the living room when the man's voice rose again.

'I don't give a tinker's cuss who this bloke is,' he declared angrily. 'He doesn't have any rights where you're concerned. For Pete's sake, Rosa, I'm your husband—'

'*Ex*-husband,' Liam thought she interjected, but the man continued as if she hadn't spoken.

'Don't I deserve some consideration? I thought we'd agreed to try and start again.'

Liam didn't hear Rosa's answer. Instead of going in search of the voices, he was now standing motionless, his shoulders pressed against the wall of the hall. So he'd been right, he thought. She *had* been expecting another visitor. Her ex-husband, no less. His jaw clamped savagely. What kind of game was she playing? The poor guy sounded as if she'd fed him the same line she'd fed Liam.

He wanted out of here! And fast. He felt as if he'd been taken for a fool. What had she been doing? Using him to make the other guy jealous? Well, she'd succeeded on two counts. He was as sick as a parrot, too.

The voices seemed too far away to be in the living room. And he didn't kid himself that Rosa had taken the argument into the hall outside. He frowned. They had to be in the kitchen—the kitchen where he'd kissed her earlier. His stomach clenched, but he ignored it. If that was so, maybe he could grab his coat and get out before either of them was any the wiser.

He chanced a look into the room and saw he was right. Someone—Rosa, probably—had picked his coat off the floor and deposited it on a chair. The chair nearest the door, he saw with some irony. Was it her way of indicating that he had already been on his way out?

The floor creaked as he crossed it, but Rosa and her husband—*ex-husband*, what a joke!—were too engrossed in their discussion to pay any attention. Then they were silent, but although Liam tensed nothing happened. God, he wondered sickly, was he kissing her? Even though he told himself he didn't care, he still wanted to go in there and shove his fist down the other man's throat.

But common sense deterred him. Besides, as the guy had said, what right did he have to interfere in Rosa's life? He meant nothing to her and, whatever he'd imagined, she could mean nothing to him. Not really. She'd done him a favour, actually. She'd shown him that not all women were like Kayla Stevens, and that was good.

He carried his coat instead of trying to put it on, leaving the door of the apartment unlocked because to close it completely would have made too much noise.

Then, treading carefully, he made his way downstairs and out of the building. He'd made it, he thought with some relief as he stepped onto the street. Then, pulling on his overcoat, he walked away without looking back.

'What was that?'

Rosa thought she'd heard something, and, pushing Colin aside, she went into the living room. But there was no one there. The room was empty, as before. She must have imagined it, she thought. Colin being here was making her as edgy as a cat.

'So where is he, this bloke you've shacked up with?' demanded Colin unpleasantly. 'Oh, I get it.' He viewed the towelling robe she'd hastily pulled on when he knocked at the door with a scornful eye. 'I got you out of bed, didn't I? So—what? Is he keeping out of my way because he's scared I might deck him?' He sneered as he strode past her. 'Let's see who's been screwing my wife, shall we?'

'Don't you dare!'

Rosa grabbed Colin's arm, trying to stop him from going into the hall that led to the bedroom, but he wasn't deterred. 'Wakey, wakey!' he called, pressing the switch and filling her bedroom with harsh light. Then he turned in some confusion. 'There's no one here.'

Rosa wished her face was less expressive. She'd have liked to say, *Who did you expect*? but the shock she'd got was more than equal to his.

And Colin knew her too well to be deceived. 'Well, what do you know?' he said mockingly. 'He's run out on you.' His lips twisted contemptuously. 'Didn't I tell you? I'm the only man you can rely on, Rosa.'

Rosa thought she would have laughed if she hadn't felt so heartsick. She thought she knew exactly why Liam had left, and it had nothing to do with whether he was reliable or not. He must have heard them talking, and, remembering what Colin had been saying, she wanted to scream in frustration. She'd told Liam she was divorced, that she'd been divorced for over three years, yet he must have heard Colin boasting about the fact that she was still his wife.

Of course she wasn't. But if Liam had heard all their conversation it would have put some doubt in his mind. Colin was so arrogant, so smug, so sure she'd agree to go back to him. But, although she was sorry his second marriage had proved as unsuccessful as his first, there was no way she ever wanted to be with Colin again.

'Just get out,' she said now, pointing towards the door.

And, although she'd thought he was going to argue, Colin had evidently decided he'd said enough for tonight.

'Hey, the door's unlocked,' he said. 'Obviously that's how he sneaked out without us hearing him. Who is he, Rosa? Don't I have a right to know who my competition is?'

'You have no rights where I'm concerned,' Rosa retorted coldly. 'And don't come here again. As far as I'm concerned, you dropped off the face of the earth three years ago.'

Colin's jaw sagged. 'You don't mean that, Rosa.'

'Trust me—I do,' she told him, pulling the outer door open. 'I hope I never see you again.'

Colin hesitated, and she briefly wondered what she'd do if he chose to ignore her. Scream her head off, she reflected. With a bit of luck her elderly neighbour would hear her and call the police. But in the event he went of his own accord, muttering that she'd regret this for the rest of her life.

Only that you came here, she thought bitterly as she slammed the door behind him. Then, collapsing onto the sofa, she felt the tears streaming down her face. She couldn't believe the evening that had begun so marvellously had ended so disastrously. And all because she'd agreed to speak to her ex-husband when he'd called her earlier in the day.

She'd even made a special effort with her appearance because Colin was coming, she thought bitterly. She'd had a shower and put on her best underwear, just to make herself feel good. She had no feelings for Colin, but that hadn't stopped her from wanting to look her best when he saw her. She'd wanted him to wish he'd never cheated on her, even if by doing so he'd probably—no, definitely—done her a favour.

And now Liam would think the worst of her. But when Colin had knocked at the door all she'd thought about was trying to stop him from waking Liam. She hadn't even intended to invite him in, but Colin had pushed past her anyway, evidently assuming she was glad to see him.

It hadn't been until she'd explained that there was someone new in her life that he'd got so abusive, lying about why he'd come here, trying to pretend that she'd agreed to start again.

It had all been just a dreadful mistake. And it was her fault. If she'd never agreed to see Colin she wouldn't be in this position now. But, dear God! She'd had no hope of ever seeing Liam again, let alone him coming to her apartment. To think he'd driven all this way just to believe she was no better than that woman he'd been engaged to.

Of course he didn't know she knew anything about his broken engagement. However, since coming home, Rosa had combed the internet for anything she could find about him.

There was pathetically little, in spite of his success. But then, he'd said that he shunned publicity. In one interview she'd read, he claimed he let his books speak for themselves. He also maintained that authors weren't necessarily interesting people just because they had the ability to tell a good tale.

There was little about the attack that had caused his injuries either. Rosa guessed Liam's attitude had forced the press to back off. Besides, the man who'd done it had killed himself after believing he'd killed his victim. There'd been no prolonged investigation, no infamous court case. Liam had spent several weeks secluded from the public in hospital, and then returned to his penthouse apartment with a security firm to guard his privacy until he'd recovered.

His girlfriend had abandoned him publicly after he'd left the hospital, but Rosa wondered if she'd really waited that long. According to the reports, she'd left him for a South American playboy who rode polo ponies for a living. She'd professed herself heartbroken for hurting Liam, but said she loved Raimondo. It had been love at first sight and there was nothing she could do to change it.

That had made the headlines. One of the many articles made much of the fact that beautiful model Kayla Stevens had soon been seen on the arm of her new lover, Raimondo Baja.

Miss Stevens used to be the girlfriend of hot new author Liam Jameson, who recently suffered a near-fatal attack from a crazed fan. Jameson, whose first book, Hunting the Vampire, has just been optioned by Morelli Studios for a slated seven-figure sum, wasn't available for comment. But his agent, Dan Arnold, says Mr Jameson wishes the couple every happiness for the future.

I bet he did, Rosa had thought cynically, when she'd read it, but now all she could think about was that she'd let him down again. What twisted truth had he thought he'd gained from Colin's lies about her? What had he heard that had convinced him she couldn't be trusted either?

Scrubbing the tears from her cheeks, Rosa got to her feet. She shouldn't sit here feeling sorry for herself. She should do something about it. But what could she do, short of getting dressed and going looking for him? And that would surely be a wasted effort. She had no idea where he might go—except as far away from her as possible, she appended bitterly.

She didn't know where he might spend the night. She didn't even have the castle's phone number. And there was no way she could desert her responsibilities and go looking for him. She was due in school again tomorrow, at eight-thirty sharp.

Leaving the living room, she went through to the bedroom, looking about the room that had been such a heavenly haven an hour ago and now looked as abandoned as she felt. She stood in the doorway, blinking back another bout of tears, and then went into the room and flung herself on the bed.

Burying her face in the pillow, she could still detect his scent, a mixture of some citrusy fragrance and the clean male scent of his body. And something else: the disturbing aroma of sex.

How was she going to get over this? She felt as if she'd been hollowed out inside so that she was totally bare, totally bereft.

She didn't need to pretend any more, she thought. She was in love with him. In love with Liam. And how futile was that?

And then a name crept into her mind. Dan, she recalled, pushing herself up from the pillows with a feeling of excitement. Dan Arnold. Yes, that was it. Dan Arnold. Liam's agent. Surely he would know Liam's phone number? And, although she didn't hold out any hope of him giving it to her, he might be prepared to give Liam a message from her.

Flinging back the covers, she thrust her feet to the floor and stood up, only to groan in pain as her toes encountered something hard and unyielding beneath the sheet. Wincing, she pulled the sheet aside, prepared to see one of the shoes she'd discarded earlier. But it wasn't a shoe. It was a mobile phone.

Feeling peeved, Rosa bent to pick up the offending article with impatient fingers. 'Damn thing,' she muttered to herself, taking a moment to massage her bruised toes. What the devil was her phone doing on the floor in here?

And then she realised it wasn't her phone at all. Goodness, she was so stupid! This had to be Liam's phone. *Liam's*. It must have fallen out of his pocket when he'd tossed his jacket on the floor. Evidently his lack of contact on the island didn't prevent him from carrying a cellphone on the mainland.

'Oh, my God,' she whispered, sinking down onto the side of the bed again. He probably used this phone to ring his agent and his publisher and anyone else he needed to get in touch with when he was travelling. In her hands, she probably held the means to solve her problem. Was it really going to be that easy?

The phone had been turned off, she saw, and now, taking a breath, she turned it on. Immediately a screensaver of the castle appeared, before clearing again to reveal the fact that Liam had three messages.

Three messages! Rosa wet her suddenly dry lips. Dared she access them? Dared she take the chance that one of them might be from Dan Arnold?

Yes!

Dialling the required number, she waited in anticipation for the first recorded message to be replayed. 'Liam?' she heard an unfamiliar woman's voice say. 'Where the hell are you? I thought you told me you'd be checking into the Moriarty at about half-past seven. It's past eight o'clock now, and I've been sitting in your suite for the past hour. Give me a ring when you get this, there's a sweetie. You know I worry about you.'

Rosa cancelled the call at that point. Now she was the one who felt stupid. She'd thought Liam had come to see *her*, when in fact she'd evidently just been an afterthought. He must have decided to call in on her on his way to London to meet this other woman. And whether she was his mother, his sister, or his girlfriend—she shuddered—she'd totally misunderstood his reasons for coming to Ripon.

Not caring if she broke it or not, Rosa flung the phone across the room and, getting off the bed, started stripping the covers from it. She wanted no trace of Liam Jameson left in this apartment, she told herself savagely.

Only when the bed was remade with clean sheets did she again give way to the scalding tears that had never been far away...

CHAPTER THIRTEEN

'WELL, I THINK you're crazy!'

Lucy Fielding turned from making her brother a cup of coffee in the state-of-the-art kitchen of the suite, and gave him an impatient look.

'You're entitled to your opinion, of course,' said Liam tightly, giving in to the temptation to lift his aching leg onto the sofa beside him. He glanced behind him. 'Isn't that coffee ready yet?'

Lucy pursed her lips, but she obediently poured a mug of dark Americano from the jug and carried it across to him. 'There you are.'

'Thanks.' Although Liam's system was already buzzing with the amount of caffeine he'd consumed in the last few hours, he made a play of taking a hungry mouthful from the mug Lucy had given him. 'Yeah, that's good.'

Lucy acknowledged his thanks with a careless shrug of her shoulders, and then came to sit on the opposite end of the sofa so that he was forced to face her. 'Not that I consider coffee an adequate substitute for breakfast,' she added reprovingly. 'But it's such a relief to see you I'm prepared to be generous.'

'Gee, thanks.' Liam looked at her from beneath his lashes. 'Sorry you had to wait so long.'

'So you should be.' Lucy shook her head. 'You know when you rang I was considering phoning the police and asking if there'd been an accident on the motorway.'

'Yeah, well, I explained about that, didn't I?' said Liam ruefully. He'd realised he'd lost his mobile phone just after he'd got onto the M1. 'I had to wait until I reached a service area before I could call.'

'Okay.' Lucy inclined her head. 'And I was so relieved to hear from you I'd have forgiven you anything then.'

'What, and you've changed your mind now?' suggested her brother mildly. 'Well, tough.'

'I didn't say that.' Lucy sighed. 'As Mike's away until Friday, I'd planned on spending the night in town.' She paused. 'So, tell me again: you say you took a detour to see some woman you met in August and her husband turned up—is that right?'

Liam's expression darkened. 'I don't want to talk about it.'

'I think you should.' Lucy regarded him closely. 'What's going on, Lee? There's more to this than what you've told me. How did you meet her, anyway? I thought you didn't take women to Kilfoil.'

'I don't.'

'So what was she doing there?'

Liam expelled a weary breath. 'Looking for her sister.'

'On the island? Or at the castle?'

'Both,' said Liam flatly, wishing he hadn't asked for the coffee now. It was too hot to swallow in one gulp, and politeness forbade him from just leaving it after Lucy had taken the trouble to make it. 'Forget it, Lucy, please.'

Lucy's lips tightened. 'I can't,' she told him shortly. 'You forget, I was around when Kayla walked out on you, and I don't like the idea that some other woman has been playing you for a fool.'

Liam groaned. 'Rosa's not like that,' he said wearily, tipping his head back against the cushions.

'So what *is* she like?'

'Tall, slim, red-haired.'

Lucy snorted. 'That's not what I meant and you know it, Lee. What's she like really? Is she like Kayla?'

'She's nothing like Kayla,' he said forcefully, looking at her again. 'I wouldn't insult her by using her name in the same breath as Kayla Stevens.'

'Kayla *Baja*,' Lucy corrected him drily. 'Who, by the way, is back in London. I've heard that she and Raimondo have split, and she's been telling anyone who'll listen to her that you're the only man she's ever loved.'

Liam gave her an incredulous look. 'You're kidding?'

Lucy shook her head. 'No, I'm serious. She cornered me in Harrods the other day and asked me if I'd seen you recently.' She smiled. 'Naturally I let her think we were seldom out of one another's pockets. I didn't think it was wise to tell her that we only see you a couple of times a year.'

Liam pulled a face. 'You know where I live.'

'But you're not exactly accessible, are you?' Lucy protested. 'And you hardly come down to London anymore.'

Liam sighed. 'I'm a writer, Lucy. I do work, you know.'

'I know.' Lucy hesitated. 'And Kayla?'

'Kayla can go—screw herself,' said Liam, moderating his language for his sister's sake. 'I don't care if I never see her again.'

And it was true, he thought incredulously. For so long

he'd avoided talking about Kayla, even thinking about Kayla, but suddenly he didn't care what anyone said. Whatever hold Kayla had had over him was gone. He could think of her now without either pain or regret. He shook his head at the feeling of freedom it gave him.

'I'm pleased to hear it,' remarked Lucy, her smile appearing. 'Obviously Rosa—what is it you said she was called? Channing? No, Chantry. Yeah, Rosa Chantry—obviously she must have something none of the others have had.'

Depression descended abruptly. 'Leave it, Lucy.'

'How can I leave it?' She stared at him frustratedly. 'Didn't she tell you she was married?'

'She's not married,' muttered Liam reluctantly. 'Or at least I don't think she is.'

'What?' Lucy blinked. 'But you said—'

However, Liam had had enough. Thrusting his half-empty mug of coffee onto the low table in front of him, he got heavily to his feet. 'I need a shower,' he said grimly, cutting her off with a sweeping movement of his hand across his throat. 'Then I want to speak to Dan before I go and see Aaron Pargeter. You're welcome to stay here, if you want to. But don't expect me to entertain you today.'

'So what's new?' said Lucy in a cool voice. 'But I might stay another night, if that's okay with you. You still owe me dinner.'

Liam regarded her with an expression that mingled affection with irritation. 'Okay,' he said, in an entirely different tone. 'Dinner tonight it is. So long as you promise not to tell me how to run my life.'

Lucy's face cleared. 'Bastard,' she said succinctly, and Liam was smiling when he left the room.

* * *

The next couple of days were bloody.

Rosa wasn't sleeping well, and although her mother had called a couple of times, asking her to go round for a meal, Rosa didn't think she could be civil to Sophie in her present frame of mind.

Her sister had abandoned her course at university about a month after the start of the autumn semester. It was too dull, too boring, she'd told Rosa and her mother. It wasn't what she'd expected, she said, and she was presently filling in at an advertising agency in Harrogate, who apparently considered her appearance more than compensation for her lack of experience.

Rosa had to admit the job suited her. Occupying the reception desk, she was the perfect image the agency wanted to promote. And, although Sophie would probably get bored with that, too, in time, for the moment she was content.

Nevertheless, that didn't make Rosa any more enthusiastic about spending an evening listening to her boast about how important her job was. Particularly as every time she saw Sophie she couldn't help thinking about Liam and what she'd lost. It had been bad enough before, but it was much worse now. She didn't even want to think about what had happened—or admit, if only to herself, that she'd known all along it couldn't last.

Wasn't that what she'd told him, for heaven's sake? Wasn't it she who'd promised him she expected no commitment from him? Maybe she was just kidding herself by thinking it was what he'd heard Colin say that had driven him away. Maybe all he'd wanted was a one-night-stand, a little diversion on his way to London.

She didn't know where the other woman came in, of course. All she could think was that she must be very tolerant if she didn't object to him indulging in a quickie on his way to meet her. Anyway, at least the woman had given her an address to send the phone to. Despite its being slightly chipped, she'd mailed the phone to Liam via the Moriarty Hotel the following day.

It didn't help that when she came out of school on Friday evening she found Colin Vincent waiting for her. He was standing beside her car, and judging by his pinched expression he'd been waiting in the cold for some time.

'What do you want?' Rosa asked, not in the mood to be charitable. She felt tired—drained, actually—and was looking forward to the weekend and a chance to catch up on her sleep.

'You're not very friendly,' said Colin resentfully, as she tossed the bags containing the work she would have to do at home onto the back seat. 'I thought you might have cooled off by now.'

'Cooled off?' Rosa stared at him.

'Calmed down, then,' amended Colin impatiently. 'Look, can we go somewhere to talk?'

Rosa gasped. 'We don't have anything to talk about, Colin,' she said. 'I thought I made my position perfectly clear. I don't want to see you again.'

Colin's jaw jutted. 'But you don't mean that.'

'Don't I?'

'No.' He was obviously searching for the right words. 'Look—I know who that bloke was, okay? The one who ran out on you. Sophie told me.'

'Sophie?' Rosa was stunned.

'Yeah.' Colin shifted a little uneasily. 'I mean, after you threw me out the other night I knew there had to be some explanation. So earlier on today I gave Sophie a ring.'

Rosa stared at him. 'You know where she works?'

'Oh, sure.' Colin grimaced. 'One of the guys at the garage told me. Terry Hadley. Do you remember him? He works in—'

'I don't give a damn where some *guy at the garage* works,' Rosa interrupted him angrily. 'But I would like to know how he knows Sophie.'

Colin looked down at his feet. 'Well, she's been seeing him, hasn't she?'

'*Seeing* him?'

'Going out with him, then,' muttered Colin tersely. 'For heaven's sake, Rosa, don't you know anything?'

'Obviously not.' Rosa shook her head. The last she'd heard, Sophie was still involved with Mark Campion. 'How long has this been going on?'

Colin looked sulky now. 'Does it matter? Since she got back from university, I suppose. She's big girl, Rosa. She doesn't need your permission.'

'No.'

Rosa's lips tightened, but she said nothing more, simply pulled open her door and slid into the driving seat.

'Hey!' Colin caught the door when she would have closed it. 'What about me?'

'What about you?'

'Come on, Rosa. When am I going to see you again?'

Rosa started the car. 'Never, I hope.'

'I don't believe you.' Colin refused to let go of the door. 'I mean, come on. This guy you met in Scotland—Liam Jameson—you don't seriously expect to see him again?'

'No.' It hurt, but Rosa had to be honest. With herself as much as him.

'There you are, then. Hell,' he snorted, 'the guy's a bloody millionaire! I dare say he could have any woman he wanted. You're attractive, Rosa, I know that, but you're not in the same league as the women he mixes with. Have you ever seen a picture of that model he was engaged to?' He rolled his eyes. 'She is one hot cookie!'

'Oh, go away, Colin,' said Rosa wearily, amazed that his words should upset her as much as they did. He was like a petulant child, she thought, and he was almost thirty-seven. 'I've told you. I don't want to see you again. What more do you want me to say?'

'Yeah, what more do you want her to say, Colin?' asked a low, harsh voice she'd never expected to hear again. 'Get lost, why don't you? While you still can.'

Rosa turned off the engine and sprang disbelievingly out of the car. But before she could speak, Colin muscled forward.

'Who the hell do you think you're talking to?' he demanded, his face turning an unpleasant shade of red. 'This is a private conversation. Why don't you get lost before I stick my fist in your face?'

'In your dreams,' said Liam mildly, his eyes moving briefly to Rosa before returning to the other man. 'On your way, Colin. I'm afraid I don't know your surname, but I guess I can live with that.'

Rosa was horrified. She knew only too well that Colin had an ugly temper. And, looking at Liam, leaning casually against the rear door of the small saloon, she could only think how vulnerable he was.

But that didn't stop her from drinking in the sight of him like a dying woman in the desert. He was wearing his long overcoat again, open now, to allow him to tuck his fingers under his arms. His feet were crossed at the ankle, and in spite of the anxiety she was feeling he looked the picture of complacency. Too complacent to be facing a man who was used to using his fists to get his way.

Colin seemed not to know how to take Liam. But his attitude had turned truculent and he moved aggressively towards the other man. 'Who do you think you are, talking to me like that?' he snarled. 'I'll go when I feel like it, and not before.'

'Your call,' said Liam carelessly, his green eyes moving back to Rosa with seeming indifference to any threat Colin posed. 'Hi,' he said, addressing her for the first time, and all Rosa's insides turned fluid. 'You look tired,' he added huskily. 'Has this joker been getting you down?'

Rosa's lips parted, but before she could speak Colin lunged forward and grabbed the lapels of the other man's coat. 'Who are you calling a joker?' he growled, pushing his face into Liam's, using every move, every gesture, to intimidate. 'Come on, talk to me, Mr Big-Time! You're not so mouthy now, are you?'

'Colin—'

'You think?' Rosa's cry of protest went unheard as Liam turned his gaze back to Colin's, with no trace of fear in the mocking smile he gave him. 'We're not all morons, you low-life. We don't all have to threaten violence to prove our masculinity.'

Rosa groaned. Liam was being deliberately provoking, and she knew exactly what her ex-husband would do.

'Why, you—'

Colin's arm drew back, but before he could deliver the punch he obviously intended, Liam's fist connected with his midriff. Rosa heard the sickening sound of bone against yielding flesh, and then Colin had to let go of Liam's coat to bend double, gasping for breath.

'You—you bastard,' he choked, when he could speak again, but Liam looked unperturbed.

'I've been called worse,' he remarked, straightening away from the car. 'Do you want to try again?'

'God, no!' Rosa cried, putting herself between them. 'This is a school, for heaven's sake. What kind of an example are you setting the kids?'

'The kids are long gone,' said Liam flatly, turning to her. 'Or are you saying you feel sorry for this—?'

He refrained from using the word that trembled on his tongue, but Rosa quickly shook her head. 'You know I'm not,' she exclaimed, her tongue running helplessly over her dry lips. 'But—but what are you doing here? I sent your phone to the hotel. Didn't you get it?'

'Screw the phone,' said Liam, putting his arm across her shoulders and pulling her towards him. 'Come here,' he muttered thickly, and, uncaring that Colin was staring at them now, with bitter, impotent eyes, he kissed her.

'For God's sake, Rosa,' Colin exclaimed angrily, but she hardly heard him.

'Get lost, Colin,' she whispered dreamily, when Liam lifted his head. 'Can't you see you're wasting your time here?'

Colin glared at her. 'You'll regret this, Rosa.'

'Oh, I hope not,' said Liam, walking her round the car and putting her into the passenger seat before taking his own seat behind the wheel. He looked up at the other man. 'Why don't you go and cry on Sophie's shoulder? She sounds just your—bag, hmm?'

Colin hadn't expected that, and he turned scandalised eyes in Rosa's direction 'Did you hear that?' he demanded, grabbing the door again. 'Rosa, did you hear what he called your sister?'

Rosa looked up at him. 'I think he was talking about you, Colin,' she said with a giggle as Liam gave an uncontrollable snort of laughter. 'Bye.'

Yet, despite what had happened, they were both oddly quiet as Liam drove the small car off the school's premises. It was as if Colin had provided a conduit between them, and now that he was gone neither of them could think of what to say.

Liam broke the silence. 'Which way?' he asked. They'd reached the main road, which was busy at this hour of the afternoon. 'I haven't got the first idea of how to get to your place from here.'

Rosa glanced at him. 'Don't you remember?' she asked tentatively, and Liam grimaced.

'If you mean the other night, I walked from the market square,' he told her, taking his chance and turning into the stream of traffic. 'So—this way, right?'

'Right,' she agreed, wishing she'd known he'd had no transport on Tuesday evening. Maybe if she'd got dressed straight away and gone after him, she could have—

Could have what? she wondered, arresting the thought almost as soon as it was formed. Just because he was here it didn't mean he hadn't lied to her in the past. He'd let her think he'd come all the way from Kilfoil to see her, when in fact he'd been on his way to London to see someone else. Another woman. How did she know he wasn't on his way to Scotland now, and had decided to call in for another quickie on the way back?

'What's wrong?'

Liam had sensed her sudden withdrawal, the moment when her mood had changed from being pleased to see him to one of wary distrust. In the excitement of seeing him again she'd obviously forgotten how they'd parted. What was she thinking at this moment? he wondered. That they'd been together before and he'd let her down?

'What are you doing here?' she asked at that moment, her gaze fixed on the lights of the cars ahead of them. 'And where's your car? Don't tell me you've left it in the market place again?'

'I didn't use a car,' Liam told her, trying to keep his mind on his driving. 'My pilot has a pal who owns a farm near Ripley. He dropped me off there, and his pal ferried me into town.'

Rosa couldn't help turning to stare at him then. 'Are we talking about your helicopter?' At Liam's nod, she went on, 'I thought you preferred your car.'

'I do, usually,' he conceded. 'But this way was easier and quicker. I've got to go back to London again tomorrow.'

Rosa swallowed her chagrin. 'Tomorrow,' she echoed blankly. And then, because she couldn't help herself, 'I don't know why you bothered coming here at all.'

Liam swore under his breath. This wasn't the sort of conversation he wanted to have when he was in control of an automobile. Dammit, it was a lethal weapon, and he had hoped they could get back to her place before starting a post mortem on his shortcomings. He knew he'd let her down. He'd let himself down. And he only had a limited number of hours to convince her he wouldn't do it again.

'You know why I came,' he said between his teeth. 'Haven't I proved it?'

'How?' Rosa was scornful. 'By punching Colin before he could punch you?'

'I won't dignify that with an answer,' he retorted, reaching another junction and glancing frustratedly up and down the busy road. 'Which way?' he asked again, and Rosa told him. 'Just save it, will you?' he added, as he took a chance and had a horn blown at him for his pains. He raised a finger in salute and put his foot on the accelerator. 'This is awfully bad for my image. I'm usually such a considerate driver.'

'Why do I find that hard to believe?' she asked provokingly, but Liam had got over his spurt of anger.

'Because you don't know me very well yet,' he said, taking one hand off the wheel to lay it on her thigh. And although she flinched away, he gripped the firm flesh above her knee with hard fingers. 'Don't worry,' he added huskily. 'You soon will.'

'Like the woman who was waiting for you at your hotel in London?' exclaimed Rosa painfully, and Liam was obliged to take his eyes off the road to give her a searing look.

'How do you—? Rosa, that was my sister,' he muttered incredulously. 'Surely you didn't think—?' He broke off again, forced to turn his attention back to the road. He gripped the wheel like a lifeline, and she saw his knuckles whiten in the light from the dash. 'Lucy is my sister,' he said again, harshly. 'Don't say another word until we get to your apartment.'

CHAPTER FOURTEEN

LIAM HAD TO PARK the car farther down Richmond Road, there being no vacant space in front of number 24. While he was getting out and locking the vehicle, Rosa hurried back to her gate.

She'd already opened the door and run up the stairs to her apartment before she heard Liam slogging up the stairs behind her. Obviously he was still having trouble with his leg, and it was an effort not to turn and offer him her help.

He wouldn't have wanted it, she assured herself, switching on the lights and turning up the thermostat on the wall. But all the time she was accomplishing these mundane tasks, the words *my sister* kept buzzing around in her head. Was that really who she'd heard? His sister? She wanted to believe it, she really did, but could she bear it if he was lying and hurt her again?

Liam entered the apartment with some relief, allowing the door to swing closed behind him and sagging back against it. Then, when he caught Rosa watching him from the kitchen doorway, he said, with an attempt at self-mockery, 'Getting old, hmm?'

Rosa pressed her lips together, but although she looked as if she didn't believe him, she didn't contradict him.

Instead, she slipped her leather coat off her shoulders and said stiffly, 'Why don't you sit down?'

'Yeah, why don't I?' he agreed, limping to the sofa and dropping down gratefully onto it. He looked up at her enquiringly, 'Why don't you join me?'

Rosa hesitated, but then she shook her head. 'Wouldn't you like a drink?' she asked, in that same unnatural voice. 'You must be cold.'

'Believe me, cold is something I'm not,' he assured her flatly. 'Come on, Rosa. Come and sit down. You know you want to.'

'Do I?'

For a moment her temper flared, and Liam's eyes darkened with sudden impatience. 'If the way you kissed me earlier is anything to go by, then I'd say yes,' he said harshly. 'Look, I know you're suspicious of me. Well, I don't blame you after the way I've behaved. But we're not going to resolve anything if you persist in behaving like an outraged virgin!'

Rosa was indignant. 'Is that supposed to make me want to forgive you?' she asked scornfully. 'Because I have to tell you, it's not working.'

'Oh, Rosa!' Liam sighed. 'Don't make me have to come after you.'

Still she didn't move. 'It's not my fault if your leg's painful,' she retorted unsympathetically, and Liam wanted to grab her and make her admit that she was just as glad to see him as he was to see her.

Instead, he said, 'It is, actually.'

Rosa gasped. 'I didn't ask you to drive from one end of the country to the other.'

'No.' Liam conceded the point. 'But that's not why I've had to check in to the clinic in London again.'

Rosa stared at him now. 'What?'

'I said—'

'I know what you said.' She took a couple of tentative steps towards the sofa. 'What clinic? What are you talking about?'

Liam sighed, closing his eyes for a moment. 'Do we have to talk about this now?'

'Yes.' Rosa nodded. 'Tell me.'

Liam opened his eyes again. 'Come and sit down, then.'

'Not until tell me what you mean. About it being my fault.'

'Oh, God!' Liam groaned. 'Well, I guess, strictly speaking, it was my own fault that I got caught in the storm.'

Rosa frowned. 'You mean, before I left the island?'

'Yeah.' Liam patted the seat beside him. 'Come on, Rosa. I promise I won't touch you if you don't want me to.'

Rosa stayed where she was. 'Tell me about the clinic first,' she said. 'What kind of clinic is it?'

Liam shrugged. 'The kind that deals with people who've been physically disabled in some way.' He paused, and when she still made no move to join him, he went on, 'When I was—attacked...' He paused again, and then added wearily, 'Do you know about that?'

'Only that some crazy guy tried to kill you.'

'Well, that about sums it up, actually.' Liam gave a short, mirthless laugh. 'This guy—his name was Craig Kennedy, by the way—he apparently confused me with one of my characters—'

'Luther Killian?' Rosa looked surprised.

'No. Not Killian. A rogue vampire called Jonas Wilder, who'd made a lot of money out of horror fiction.' He pulled a wry face. 'I guess you get the connection.'

'And he thought you were this Jonas Wilder?'

'In the flesh,' agreed Liam drily. 'The anti-Christ personified.' But, although he was trying to make light of it, Rosa could see the dark shadows that still lingered in his eyes when he spoke of it. 'Happily, he was less successful at achieving his ends than Luther.'

'Oh, Liam.' Rosa came towards him now, dropping down onto the sofa beside him and taking one of his hands in both of hers. 'You must have been terrified!'

Liam grimaced. 'I guess I was too shocked at the time to feel anything but disbelief. The medics said I must have put up a fight because of the defensive injuries I sustained. I remember him lashing out at me, screaming that he was going to rid the world of another monster.' He forced a smile. 'Ironically, he was using a steel blade. Any vampire freak could have told him that you need a wooden stake, driven through the heart, to destroy a vampire.'

Rosa caught her breath. 'That's not funny.'

'Hey, I know that.' Liam regarded her with rueful eyes. 'I'm no hero, Rosa. I had pretty horrific nightmares for— well, for months after it happened.'

'Oh, Liam!' She lifted his hand and pressed her lips to his knuckles, and he saw the tears glistening in her eyes. 'It must have been awful.'

Liam gave a concessionary nod, but he withdrew his hand from hers. 'It wasn't good,' he agreed. 'But I don't want your pity.'

'It's not pity,' she protested, staring at him. 'I just don't know what to say, that's all.'

Liam took a deep breath. 'You could say you're pleased to see me,' he remarked after a moment, and Rosa's shoulders rounded in defeat.

'You know I am,' she said huskily. 'But—but when I thought you'd just called here on your way to London to see another woman—'

'I was on my way to the clinic, actually.' Liam sighed. 'I didn't tell you because it's not something I'm particularly proud of.'

Rosa supposed she could understand that, although as far as she was concerned he had nothing to be ashamed of. 'And did you?' she asked instead. 'Check yourself into the clinic?'

'Yesterday,' he agreed. 'Then I checked myself out again this morning and flew up here. But I have to go back.'

'Oh!' Rosa nodded. 'That's what you meant when you said you had to go back to London tomorrow.'

'Yeah.' Liam considered her pale face. 'Do you believe me?'

'Of course.'

'There's no "of course" about it,' retorted Liam. 'A little while ago you were accusing me of going to London to see another woman.' He frowned. 'How did you get to speak to Lucy anyway? She never said she'd had a call from you.'

Rosa gasped. 'Does she know about me?'

'Oh, yes.'

'You told her?'

'She wheedled it out of me,' said Liam drily. 'My sister is nothing if not determined.'

'Gosh!' Rosa's cheeks turned pink.

'*Gosh?*' Liam gazed at her disbelievingly. 'My God, I've never heard anybody actually use that expression before. Do you say "goodness" and "oh, bother," too?'

Rosa stared at him for a moment, as if she didn't know

how to take him, and then she realised he was just teasing her. 'Oh, you!' she exclaimed, punching his arm but without any real desire to hurt him, and Liam caught her hand and pulled her against him.

'That's better,' he said, his voice thickening with satisfaction. Then his mouth found hers, and for a long time he didn't say anything at all.

His kiss was hot and hungry, showing her in so many ways that only her recalcitrance and his self-restraint had kept them apart this long. He seemed starved for her, his hand sliding into her hair, angling her face to make it easier for him to deepen and lengthen what had become a wholly carnal possession. The erotic slide of his tongue against hers caused her to tremble uncontrollably, and she fumbled her arms around his neck and clutched a handful of his hair.

'This was worth coming back for,' Liam groaned, shifting to accommodate the sudden bulge between his legs. He sucked on her lower lip, biting her and tasting her, drawing the tip of her tongue between his teeth. 'And I was afraid you'd never want to see me again.'

'You didn't really think that,' whispered Rosa, tugging his ears reprovingly. 'Or you wouldn't be here.'

'No.' He conceded the point, and she thought he never looked more attractive than when he was pretending to be chastened. 'Still, you can probably thank Lucy for part of that.'

'Lucy?' Rosa drew back to rest her forehead against his. 'Your sister?'

'For her sins.' He nodded. 'It was she who helped persuade me that I was behaving like an idiot.'

Rosa's eyes widened. 'How did she do that?'

'The way she usually does things,' said Liam wryly. 'She keeps on and on about something until you're compelled to tell her what she wants to know if only to shut her up.'

'And she wanted to know about me?'

Liam gave her a measured look. 'As if you didn't know.'

Rosa dimpled. 'Go on. I want to hear what she had to say.'

'Yeah, well—' Liam pulled back now, cradling her face between his palms. 'Before I tell you, perhaps you'd like to explain how you found out about Lucy?'

'Oh…' Rosa sighed. 'Can't you guess?'

'Humour me.'

'All right. All right.' She sighed again. 'If you insist on having your pound of flesh, I listened to the message she'd left on your phone.'

'Ah.' Liam's lips twitched. 'That wouldn't have anything to do with the fact that when I got the phone back it was chipped in several places?'

Rosa gave him a defiant look. 'You noticed?'

'Oh, yeah.' Liam's thumbs stroked across her cheekbones, a sensuous caress that caused a shiver of helpless anticipation to slide down her spine. 'Lucy pointed it out to me.'

'And I suppose you both had a good laugh about it?' said Rosa accusingly, but Liam shook his head.

'No.' His jade eyes darkened. 'It gave me the courage to come back here and find out if you were just bugged because I ran out on you or because of something else.'

Rosa shrugged. 'Like what?'

'Like—well, having listened to Lucy's message myself, I had to admit it could be—misconstrued.'

Rosa swallowed. 'So now you know why I thought you were going to meet another woman?'

'Yeah, I know.'

'And I suppose you think it was lucky that Colin was there this afternoon when you came to meet me.'

Liam gave her a strange look. 'I wouldn't put it quite like that.'

'No, but it saved you having to ask me if I was still seeing him,' Rosa declared tremulously. 'I mean, when you walked out of the apartment you obviously thought I'd been lying—'

'Don't!' Liam moved one hand to cover her mouth, preventing her from going on. 'Don't, baby,' he said again, his eyes full of compassion. 'I don't need you to tell me what a fool I've been. God, I've been regretting not giving you a chance to explain what was going on ever since I left.' He paused, removing his hand and briefly replacing it with his lips before continuing, 'But try and understand, if you can. I know my faults, better than anyone. I know I'll never win any beauty competitions. And I dare say you heard that the girl I was engaged to when I was attacked walked out on me when she discovered that, as well as looking like a monster, I might not be able to function as a man anymore.'

Rosa gasped. 'You *don't* look like a monster. And—and you can—you know—'

She broke off and Liam grinned. 'Oh, yeah,' he said humorously. 'You know I'm not impotent. But as for the rest—'

'Liam, you're the only one who sees your injuries as anything more than a few fading scars,' Rosa protested huskily. She lifted a finger and tapped his temple. 'They've gone from your body, but you're still keeping them in here.' She leaned towards him and kissed his forehead. 'You've got to let them go. They don't matter, believe me. Not to me. Not to any woman worth her salt.'

'Well, as you're the only woman I care about, I suppose I'll have to believe you,' he murmured, nuzzling her neck. 'But, if I'm honest, I'll admit I *was* glad to see your ex again.'

Rosa frowned. 'You were?'

'Yeah.' Liam's grin deepened. 'If you must know, I've been itching to smack that bastard ever since he came to the apartment. Still,' he added smugly, 'I think he got the message.'

Rosa felt a smile lurking at the corner of her own lips. 'He got the message,' she confirmed. 'And there was I, worried sick that he might hurt you.'

'Hey, after I was on my feet again, I attended a course on self-defence,' said Liam comfortingly. 'Hopefully, I'll never have to face another maniac with a knife, but, compared to Craig Kennedy, Colin was a piece of cake.'

'So I noticed.' Rosa slipped her arms around his neck again. 'Now, are you going to take off your coat?'

'I will if you will,' he replied teasingly, his fingers slipping beneath the hem of the sweater she'd worn to school. Then he groaned. 'I should have known it wasn't going to be that simple.'

'What do you mean?'

Liam shucked his overcoat and jacket off his shoulders. 'See—I'm just wearing a shirt.' He grimaced. 'I don't know how many layers you're wearing.'

'As it happens, it's cold in the classroom,' said Rosa indignantly. 'And I'm only wearing a vest under my blouse.'

'Only!' Liam was mocking. 'So—take them off.'

Rosa drew a shaky breath. 'Now?' She glanced towards the door. 'Don't you want to go into the bedroom?'

'Not particularly.' Liam's eyes were dark and undeniably sexy. 'I think we should christen the sofa instead.'

Rosa's breathing quickened. 'You shouldn't say things like that,' she exclaimed reprovingly. 'What if someone comes?'

Liam arched dark brows. 'Are you expecting anyone?'

'N-o.'

'All right.'

Rosa's tongue circled dry lips. She could do this, she told herself. Even though she'd never done a striptease for any man, least of all Colin. Her ex-husband had always behaved as if sex was something you did in bed and nowhere else, and she wondered now whether that had been his fault or hers.

Her fingers went to the hem of her sweater and, taking a deep breath, she hauled it over her head. Her hair was probably all over the place now, she thought, but, refusing to worry about it, she started on the buttons of her blouse.

However, she was all thumbs, and after watching her struggling for several tense seconds Liam brushed her hands aside and tackled the job himself.

But the buttons proved just as resistant to his efforts as they'd done to hers, and after a moment Liam gave up. Taking hold of the neckline, he simply tore it open. 'That's better.'

Rosa blinked at him. 'You didn't have to destroy it.'

'I'll buy you another,' he said carelessly. 'Something equally as unflattering, if that's what you want.'

Rosa bit her lip. 'You're too impatient.'

'I'm getting there,' he agreed mildly. He fingered the hem of her vest. 'Does this have buttons, too?'

'You know it doesn't.' Rosa was finding it increasingly difficult to breathe at all. Pulling the vest over her head, she cast it and the blouse aside. 'Satisfied?'

'By no means,' he murmured wryly. Then, flicking the

elasticated strap of her bra, he added. 'You didn't say anything about this.'

Rosa trembled. 'I'm sure you know how to take one of these off.'

'I'm sure I do, too, but I want you to do it.' His eyes caressed her. 'Please.'

Rosa shook her head, but her hands went obediently behind her back to release the catch. When the loosened straps tipped off her shoulders Liam completed the job by pulling them off her arms.

'Beautiful,' he said, just looking at her, and Rosa forgot all about being self-conscious in the sensual warmth of his eyes.

He put out his hands and gripped her bare midriff, but although her nipples were aching for him to touch them, he only allowed his thumbs to brush the undersides of her breasts.

His hands were faintly rough and unfamiliar, but their abrasion against her soft flesh caused a gnawing hunger down deep in her belly. She wanted him to touch her every-where, most particularly between her legs, and the waiting was becoming as intolerable to her as it had been to him.

With unsteady fingers she sought the buttons on his shirt, and he let her. Having more success with his larger buttons, she soon achieved her objective, and when she pushed the shirt off his shoulders he didn't try to stop her.

The only reaction she noticed was the sudden tenting of his pants as her fingers touched the hair that grew down the middle of his chest. And when he saw where she was looking he uttered a rueful groan.

'Yeah, yeah, now I'm impatient,' he said, giving in to the urge to lift her breasts with his hands. The swollen tips pushed provocatively against his palms and, unable to stop himself, he bent and took one into this mouth.

But it wasn't enough for either of them, and Liam's fingers fumbled with the button at the waist of her trousers.

'I'll do it,' she said breathlessly, and while she pushed her trousers and her panties down her legs, Liam did the same.

For the first time, Rosa had the opportunity to see the scar that began low on his stomach and arrowed down the inner part of his thigh.

He saw her looking, but he didn't try to cover himself. 'Ugly, isn't it?' he said roughly, half expecting to see revulsion in her face even now.

But all Rosa did was bend her head and bestow a line of kisses from the harsh gash that marked the top of the wound to the more sensitive place between his legs.

And by then Liam was breathing heavily. 'Enough,' he said unsteadily. 'I want to be inside you when I come, and unless you stop right now there are no guarantees.'

Rosa smiled. 'So what are you waiting for?' she asked, lying back on the sofa, one leg raised provocatively. She trailed a tempting hand down her body. 'I'm not going anywhere.'

EPILOGUE

SIX MONTHS LATER, Rosa stood at the bedroom window, gazing out at the view that never failed to enchant her. It was spring, and Kilfoil was just beginning to burgeon with colour. There were daffodils and tulips growing in the lee of the castle wall, and last night Sam had shown her the first shoots of the orchids that she'd discovered were his secret passion, growing in one of the hothouses he tended.

Standing here, watching the ocean that was today flecked with white foam, Rosa could hardly believe that she'd been married to Liam for over six weeks. Of course she'd been at Kilfoil since Christmas, except for the four weeks they'd spent in the Caribbean after they were married, but she felt as if she'd always lived here. Like Liam, she had no desire to live anywhere else. This was their home.

But it had been an unbelievable six months since he'd turned up at the school that afternoon. In the beginning, Rosa had been sure she must be dreaming. The fact that Liam loved her had seemed too good to be true.

Yet it wasn't.

Her family had been stunned when she'd first introduced Liam to them. Her mother had been doubtful that he could be serious about her elder daughter. 'Now, if it had been Sophie,' she'd said, in her usual unthinking way, 'I wouldn't have been surprised.'

Rosa had weathered this, as she'd weathered all her mother's unkind comments in the past, but Liam hadn't liked to see her being hurt. 'The trouble with your mother,' he'd said when they were alone, 'is that she doesn't realise that although she's got two beautiful daughters, only one of them's a real woman.'

Sophie herself had been surprisingly philosophical. Although it was in her nature to flirt with every man she met, she wasn't offended when Liam teased her about it. She'd told Rosa that she thought Liam was a real dish, and that she wished it *had* been him who'd taken her to London, instead of that creep Jed Hastings.

The only real fly in the ointment had been Kayla Stevens-Baja.

Liam had had to return to the Knightsbridge clinic, and when she'd discovered he was in London, Kayla had thrown herself on his mercy, begging him to forgive her and telling him he was the only man she'd ever really loved.

Of course Kayla had made sure it made headlines, and although Liam had been phoning Rosa every day, telling her how much he missed her, she hadn't been able to help worrying that the other woman might persuade him to go back to her.

However, a couple of days after the headlines about Kayla's visit to the clinic had appeared in the tabloids, Liam had turned up in Ripon again—this time with a ring.

Their engagement had appeared in *The Times* the following day, and although Liam would have liked Rosa to resign from her job and return to Scotland with him, he'd agreed to wait until Christmas for her to join him.

And now...

She was drawing a tremulous breath when a drowsy voice said, 'What are you doing?'

Turning, Rosa saw her husband was awake, too. Propped up on his elbows, the warm quilt loose about his lower limbs, Liam looked wonderfully tanned and relaxed, and Rosa left the window to kneel beside him on the bed.

'I was just admiring the view,' she said, aware that the filmy nightgown left little to his imagination.

'Mmm.' Liam's smile was possessive. 'I know exactly what you mean.' But he was looking at her, not towards the windows, and she pushed him playfully back against the pillows.

'You're impossible,' she said, straddling his supine body so he couldn't get up again. 'But I'm just so happy to be home I'll forgive you.'

Liam arched his dark brows. 'Didn't you enjoy our honeymoon?' he asked in a mock-wounded voice, and she pulled a face at him.

'Our honeymoon was—heavenly,' she told him contentedly. 'I loved the Caribbean. You know I did. But this is where we live.'

Liam grinned up at her. 'You know, I didn't know real redheads could go brown,' he murmured provocatively. 'But you've got a lovely peachy tan.'

Rosa caught her breath. 'Are you implying I'm not a real redhead?'

'Oh, no.' Liam's eyes dropped lower. 'I know you are. Who better?'

Rosa couldn't help herself. A faint colour touched her cheeks, and to divert him she said, 'At least I'm not the skinny creature I was when we first met.'

'No.' Liam agreed with her, his hands curving over her hips, making her intensely aware of his morning erection beneath her bottom. 'You're fattening up nicely. Mrs Wilson will be pleased.'

Rosa was horrified. 'I'm not fat, am I?' she protested, scrambling off the bed again and scurrying across to the adjoining dressing room with its long mirrored doors. 'Oh, God, I *am* getting fat!' she exclaimed, running anxious hands over her midriff. 'I've got quite a mound here.' She made a worried sound. 'I'll have to cut down on those chocolate puddings Mrs Wilson keeps tempting me with.'

Liam appeared behind her then. He was naked, and for a moment she was diverted by the muscular beauty of his body. The scars were still there, of course, but these days she hardly noticed them, and Liam himself was no longer self-conscious about being seen without clothes.

'Stop stressing,' he said, sliding his arms around her from behind and drawing her back against his still-aroused body. 'I love you just the way you are.'

Rosa shook her head. 'But I've never been fat,' she said, shivering at the sight of his hands moving over the offending curve of her stomach. He only had to touch her and she went up in flames.

'You don't think it could be something else, do you?' he suggested, his lips tracing the tender curve of her neck. He looked at her reflection in the mirror. 'I mean, you haven't been married to me before.'

Rosa caught her breath. 'What are you saying?'

'Well, we have been sleeping together for the past six

months,' he pointed out mildly. 'And, so far as I'm aware, we haven't taken any precautions.'

Rosa stared back at him. 'You think—I could be pregnant?'

Liam shrugged. 'I know you insisted that you couldn't have a baby,' he said softly, 'but I'm not convinced. My sisters have both been pregnant, and this looks awfully similar to me.'

Rosa expelled a shaken breath. Then, with tentative fingers, she explored the gentle mound below her ribcage. It did feel awfully firm to be just fat. Goodness, she thought, that was a possibility she'd never considered.

After being married to Colin for five years and never getting pregnant, she'd naturally assumed that she had been to blame.

She tried to think. How long was it since she'd had her period? She realised that she hadn't had that inconvenience for at least eight weeks. Since before she and Liam had got married, in fact. Oh, God! She trembled. Could it be true?

'You know,' went on Liam gently, 'it could have been Colin who couldn't father a child.'

Rosa turned her head to look into his eyes. 'You think?' she asked, gazing at him in wonderment, and Liam gave her a wry smile.

'Why not?' he asked smugly. 'He was no good at anything else, was he?'

A nervous giggle escaped her. 'And—if I am, how will you feel?'

'Hey, if you're happy, I'm happy,' he said huskily. 'I would have liked to have you all to myself for a little bit longer, but that's what grandparents are for, isn't it?'

'Do you think your parents will be pleased?'

Rosa had met Liam's mother and father, and his two sisters and their families, at the wedding, and she'd liked them a lot. But then, she'd thought, how could she not love the people who had made Liam the man he was?

'They'll be delighted,' he assured her firmly. 'I mean, I'm getting older all the time. The old biological clock is ticking.'

'I don't think you have anything to worry about,' said Rosa rather breathily, drawing back to admire his very prominent maleness. 'Come on, I'm getting cold here. And we have something to celebrate.'

Their son was born six and a half months later. Sean Liam Jameson was delivered—despite his father's anxiety—in the main bedroom at Kilfoil Castle, attended only by the local midwife.

Liam had made arrangements for Rosa to be airlifted by helicopter to the mainland hospital as soon as she went into labour. But unfortunately an autumn storm had stranded a group of fishermen aboard a fishing boat that was drifting without power in the North Sea. Rosa, despite a little anxiety of her own, had insisted that rescuing the fishermen was more important than taking her to the hospital. She was fit and strong and, according to the midwife, perfectly capable of delivering her child without either a doctor or a delivery suite.

And she had. The labour had been surprisingly easy, and short, and when the nurse put the baby into Liam's arms for the first time he looked absolutely stunned.

'He's so beautiful,' he said, handing her to his wife, and Rosa smiled.

'Just like his father,' she whispered, touching the baby's soft cheek, but Liam shook his head.

'You're the beautiful one,' he told her fiercely.

And, despite the fact that she was hot and tired, and soaked with sweat, Rosa knew he meant it...

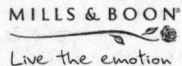

MILLS & BOON®

Live the emotion

Modern
romance™

THE RICH MAN'S ROYAL MISTRESS
by Robyn Donald

Princess Melissa Considine is captivated by womanising
billionaire Hawke Kennedy. His seduction leads the
virginal princess to decide she will let Hawke teach her
how to love…and be loved. But Melissa knows that she
must put duty before their affair…

AT THE SHEIKH'S COMMAND *by Kate Walker*

Abbie Cavanaugh can obtain her brother's freedom – but
only if she marries the Sheikh of Barakhara. The passion
between Sheikh Malik and Abbie could mean a marriage
of delight… But neither of them knows the other's real
identity, and the truth creates a desert storm…

THE SPANIARD'S PREGNANCY PROPOSAL
by Kim Lawrence

Having been burned badly before, Fleur Stewart reckons
staying away from Spanish billionaire Antonio Rochas
should be no problem. But Antonio is sexy, smouldering,
and attracts women like moths to a flame. And he doesn't
intend to let Fleur go easily…

AN ITALIAN ENGAGEMENT *by Catherine George*

Max Wingate is broodingly handsome. But his romantic
charm won't persuade Abigail Green to fall into his arms.
There's something vulnerable about Abby, but Max is
driven by desire. He's determined to have her surrender
to him, and he'll use any means at his disposal…

On sale 6th October 2006

*Available at WHSmith, Tesco, ASDA, Borders, Eason,
Sainsbury's and most bookshops*

www.millsandboon.co.uk